ALEATHA ROMIG

Book #1 of the SIN series

New York Times, Wall Street Journal, and USA
Today bestselling author of the Consequences series,
Infidelity series, Sparrow trilogies: Web of Sin,
Tangled Web, Web of Desire, and Dangerous Web,
and the Devil's Series Duet

COPYRIGHT AND LICENSE INFORMATION

RED SIN

resemblance to any actual persons, living or dead, events, or locales is entirely coincidental.

RED SIN

Prologue

Red is the color of blood, sacrifice, danger, and courage. It's also associated with heat, passion, and sexuality. When two people meet unexpectedly with an inexplicable attraction that defies common understanding...it can be called RED SIN.

Julia and Van found one another in a shaken snow globe. Stranded in a blizzard, they embraced being two individuals with no last names. The plan was to walk away from each other with no regrets—until that plan changed.

Julia's life was delivered a staggering blow the day she discovered her fiancé's infidelity. The night she met a handsome stranger, one who showed her the possibility of a life filled with more than the fulfillment of expectations, she took a chance.

When it comes to business, Donovan Sherman is a wolf—a bloodthirsty carnivore who leaves wounded prey and victims in his wake. He learned from the best, his onetime nemesis and now-mentor, Lennox Demetri, who showed him that opportunities are only ripe for those willing to risk it all, a lesson Donovan took to heart.

With Julia McGrath, Donovan must decide if this beautiful woman who showed him the meaning of red sin will fall victim as his prey or if after experiencing the unbridled passion, there is more that he wants.

From New York Times bestselling author Aleatha Romig comes a brand-new romantic-suspense novel in the world of high finance, where success is sweet and revenge is sweeter.

Have you been Aleatha'd?

Author NOTE

"WHITE RIBBON," a novella, first appeared in the no-longer-available Top Shelf Romance anthology *I HAVE LIVED AND I HAVE LOVED.*

Since the original publication, a few changes have been made to the novella.

If you have read "WHITE RIBBON," in the anthology, I recommend you begin at the beginning so as to not miss a thing. If you read "WHITE RIBBON" as a free prequel novella—where the updates were present—you may jump ahead to chapter seven.

Chapters one through six of *RED SIN* are "WHITE RIBBON" as found in the limited-release free novella.

It was my plan to avoid making you jump from here to a free prequel and back.

If you haven't read "WHITE RIBBON" anywhere else, or if you'd like to refresh your memory on how Van and Julia met in a shaken snow globe along the white ribbon, please start at chapter one.

As I first wrote "WHITE RIBBON" it became

obvious to me that I wanted more Julia and Van in my life. I knew there was much more to their story: more intrigue, more mystery, and many more sexy times to come.

I hope you feel the same way as you begin the Sin Series with book one, *RED SIN,* including where it all began on the "WHITE RIBBON."

~Aleatha

Chapter 01

Julia

My knuckles blanched on the steering wheel as I pumped the brakes of my rental car. Even though I'd been told—more than once—that automatic brakes didn't require pumping, I couldn't help myself. The action calmed my nerves, giving me the illusion that I had an ounce of control as the tires slid and scooted upon the ice-covered road and large snowflakes the size of oranges fell from the sky.

With the sheer quantity of snowflakes hitting the windshield, I knew any sense of control I thought I possessed was nothing more than a figment of my imagination. If circumstances were different, I could relax and see the beauty around me. If instead of driving alone to an unknown future, I was sipping hot chocolate next to a roaring fire with friends and family, I might be able to appreciate that I had somehow managed to enter a giant snow globe and that whole world had just been given a strong shake.

My attention went back and forth between what I believed was the road before me and my GPS. The directional system had taken me on what it considered the best route. According to the screen, I was still on the pavement; thank God the GPS could differentiate because from my viewpoint, everything between the endless borders of tall pine trees was nothing more than a white ribbon.

Though I continued forward, my estimated time of arrival continued to grow later and later. That was in no doubt due to my decreased speed. Between the snow-and-ice-covered surface, the lack of defined road, and increased blizzard conditions including gusty wind, it seemed as if instead of driving, the car was crawling forward. The speedometer varied between fifteen and a whopping twenty-five miles per hour.

When I'd left Chicago this morning, the forecast had been clear. The weathercaster said that snow wasn't supposed to arrive until late tomorrow. With only a seven-hour drive, my plan was to arrive at the hotel in Ashland, Wisconsin, before nightfall, spend a few days, and get a feel for the city. With fewer than ten thousand people, it would be drastically different from what I was used to in Chicago.

Different—that in a nutshell was exactly why I applied for this job.

"Good plan, Julia," I said aloud to myself.

Maybe after hours of driving north from Chicago, I was hungry to hear a human voice, one not singing or on a podcast. Or perhaps, I was too exasperated with my situation to keep quiet any longer.

"Did you ever wonder why this job was available? It's because whomever this client is could be a psycho and on top of that, it's located in the middle of nowhere."

Sadly, nowhere was exactly what I'd sought.

Going back to my analogy of a shaken snow globe, that was my life.

Shaken.

Hours of driving had given me a new perspective, one that benefited from a bit of distance. I knew there were many people who faced greater obstacles and more adversity. I also wasn't the princess in the ivory tower that many believed me to be.

My eyes narrowed as I tried to make out the road before me. The headlights created a tunnel of illumination filled with glistening large snowflakes above a thick white blanket.

"Come on, you can make it. Just" —I looked again at the GPS— "another hour."

My stomach growled as I held tighter to the steering wheel, feeling the way the wind gusts pushed me sideways. I shook my head, wondering if I'd see any signs of civilization: a gas station or small town. The darker the sky became as my car plowed through the accumulating snow, the more I admitted to myself that I should have stopped in the last town.

As I crept onward, the phrase 'should have' seemed to repeat on a loop in my thoughts.

I should have stopped in the last town, filled the gas tank, gotten something to eat, and found a hotel.

I should have said no to Skylar Butler when he asked me to marry him. I should have seen the writing on the wall. I should have discouraged my parents from planning the most lavish wedding of the century. I should have known his parents were more excited about our nuptials than he was. I should have questioned Skylar's schedule, his trips, and the times he didn't answer his cell phone. I should have trusted what I'd known most of our lives.

In my defense, as the sayings went, hindsight was twenty-twenty and love was blind.

In my case, I think a more accurate assessment of our impending nuptials was that our love didn't have vision problems; it quite simply never existed, not in the way that made your heart beat faster or your mouth go dry. It wasn't that Skylar wasn't easy on the eyes.

He was handsome and he knew it.

That had been an issue since we were young.

Skylar was also capable when it came to foreplay.

Further than that, and I was in the minority of women in Skylar's orbit. I didn't know if the rumors of his sexual prowess were accurate. We'd agreed to wait for that final consummation of our relationship. That's not to say we hadn't gotten close. The thing was, we'd been a couple since either of us could walk or talk. It was difficult to think of one another in romantic terms.

The agreement of remaining pure was implied.

Apparently, it was an agreement between Skylar and me, not him and...well, anyone else.

My grip intensified on the steering wheel. It wasn't the worsening conditions but the memory of finding the text message from my best friend and maid of honor, Beth.

Let me backtrack.

A year ago, at a large holiday gathering surrounded by family and friends along with some of the most powerful people in both our families' world, Skylar took my hand and on bended knee proposed. Like everything else in his life, the entire scene was a performance. My smile and acceptance weren't as important as the hushed whispers, the pregnant pause waiting for my answer, and the cheers from the crowd when I said yes.

And then my fiancé was off for cigars and bourbon with our fathers and others in the same social sphere to celebrate the uniting of our families. It wasn't as if I were forgotten. No, I now had an important role. I was immediately surrounded by our mothers and all the ladies in Chicago's high society who could welcome me into the married world of Chicago's finest.

Becoming Mrs. Skylar Butler was a destination I never questioned. The road map had been not only sketched but written in ink since the day of my birth, just three months after Skylar's.

Time moved on. My wedding showers were completed. Our newly constructed home was mostly finished, filled with gifts and all the luxuries money could buy. Our two-week overseas honeymoon trip was booked, and RSVPs to the big day were coming in by the hundreds.

Our wedding was set for New Year's Eve.

It will be—*was* to be—the event of the decade.

No expense had been spared for the union of Julia McGrath and Skylar Butler.

This was not only a love story—according to all the society pages—but the business deal of the century. My family lost majority interest in privately owned Wade Pharmaceutical before fiscal-year 2000 when our stock hold went below fifty percent. The reasons could be cited as bad management, the economy, or a number of decisions that didn't pan out. Regardless, my family lost what we'd possessed since my great-grandfather founded the company.

My family's controlling interest existed by a paper-thin margin.

Dad blamed it all on my grandfather's decision to offer shares of Wade—a privately held company—to outside investors. Over time, the chosen investors sold to others, increasing the number of investors, weakening my family's influence, and increasing liability. As was spelled out in my grandfather's will, our family's shares of Wade Pharmaceutical would transfer to me upon my fulfillment of his criteria, the final step being marriage.

The Butlers held twenty-five percent of Wade stock. By combining the Butler and McGrath stock, the founding family could once again fend off attacks from Big Pharma. It was my father's constant belief that a coup was in the works. He believed that the giants in the industry were picking up shares here, with another there, to swoop in and swallow up Wade.

With my family's thirty-nine percent and the Butlers' twenty-five, Wade would be secure.

The evening after my last bridal shower and a week before Christmas, Skylar and I were to attend a charity event at the Chicago Philharmonic. Before the performance, we drove out to our new estate, west of the city on a sprawling ten-acre plot of land— our future home.

Skylar had laid his phone on the kitchen counter before going out back to check on some last-minute construction changes. Our wedding was only two weeks away, and the house needed to be ready upon our return from our honeymoon.

When I saw my best friend's name flash on the screen of his phone, I envisioned a planned pre-wedding surprise. I justified that she'd call Skylar; after all, we'd all known one another for years and also, she was the maid of honor in our wedding.

Opening the text message, I was without a doubt surprised.

"Oh no." My scream echoed as the rental car lost its traction and began to spin, flinging me from the thoughts of the recent past to the here and now.

Still a ways from my destination, my life flashed before my eyes as the white ribbon appeared to be replaced by trees and then back to the ribbon. Like a child's top, I continued around and around.

In those visions, I saw Skylar and myself as we were growing children. I recalled my desire to pursue literature and journalism, an unacceptable major for the future owner of a pharmaceutical company. Double majoring in business and literature, I squeezed in a minor in journalism from Northwestern. The academic road took me an additional semester, allowing me to complete my degree in time for the grand engagement.

The car came to a stop, bringing me back to the present.

Letting out my held breath, I laid my forehead on

the steering wheel and closed my eyes. Opening them, I saw that I was no longer on the white ribbon of road. The hood of the car was mostly buried in a snowbank and from my vantage, it looked like the bumper must have stopped inches from a tall pine tree.

I reached for my cell phone. There was no signal.

Glancing into the rearview mirror, I saw my own blue eyes. "Happy holidays, Julia. You had a fiancé, a family, a company, and a brand-new home. Maybe you should have stayed."

Swallowing, I stared out at the white surrounding me.

With each passing minute, determination surged through my veins.

If I stayed in the car, I'd freeze.

If I began walking, I could freeze.

"You didn't get here by staying put."

It was a conversation with myself; nevertheless, it was accurate.

After learning that my best friend was expecting my fiancé's baby, I bolted from our newly constructed home, leaving Skylar stranded. As I drove away, my mind spiraled with the shock of my uncertain future. Millions of thoughts swirled in a whirlwind only to settle with no distinguishable rhyme or reason. It was as one disconnected thought passed by that I grabbed ahold, recalling a job listing I'd seen nearly a month earlier.

Pulling over outside Chicago, I searched, only to find the listing still existed. It read as follows:

Financier seeks writer to pen memoir. No experience required. Must be willing to live on-site until the project is complete. Salary negotiable. Contact Fields and Smith Agency for more information.

It was a crazy idea—a crazy idea that would allow me to walk away from my life's planned trajectory, and in the process, utilize my degree in literature and journalism. From the side of the road, I sent a message to the Fields and Smith Agency, a legal firm in Ashland, Wisconsin.

Less than an hour later, I received a phone call. The gentleman on the other end of the call sounded older. He asked all the appropriate questions. It was when I asked who the financier was that Mr. Fields informed me that his client wanted to remain anonymous until it was time to meet a candidate.

"Have I heard of this person?" I asked on the call.

"I'm not certain who you've heard of, Miss McGrath."

"Is he old? Or is he a she?"

"You will have your own quarters. My client's gender and age are irrelevant."

"Is there something wrong with your client?"

"No, miss. My client prefers his privacy, and this project is something he takes seriously. I assure you, if you are selected, you will be well compensated."

The only clue I'd managed to glean was that the client was male.

It wasn't compensation I sought. It was the chance to get away from my commitments and obligations—my shares of Wade would remain in my father's hands—and to take some time away from all the lies I'd accepted, to find out what it was I truly wanted.

"I'd like to have an interview, Mr. Fields."

"How soon can you get to Ashland?"

"In a few days."

"There is the holiday."

"I am aware, Mr. Fields, but I'd like to move on to this opportunity or to something else."

My note to my parents simply said that the wedding was canceled, and I would be in touch. Throwing clothes and cosmetics into two suitcases, I waited until morning and began to drive. Hell, I didn't even know who this client was who wanted privacy. I envisioned an old man on death's door with war stories to tell—stories he felt would be relevant to someone.

Before they'd passed, I'd been close with my grandparents. The idea of listening to some old man's stories in the middle of nowhere and writing them down wasn't unappealing. I wished I'd spent more time listening to my grandfather's stories.

Taking a deep breath, I secured my lined boots, added another layer of a down coat, and donned my gloves and hat. As I took one last look in the rearview mirror, determination continued to grow.

I was here and by God, I wasn't going to freeze to death in a car on the side of the road.

Reaching for the door handle, I opened the latch. It took pushing with my full weight, but I finally managed to wedge the door open into the snowbank.

After securing my belongings, minus my phone, in the trunk, I climbed up onto what was the road. Ducking my head from the pelting snow, I continued to follow the white ribbon.

Chapter 02

Julia

The monologue in my head lost its ferocity. My self-absorbed determination to leave my life behind became more morose as I contemplated the possibility that I had facilitated that very goal—leaving my life, not by choice but by death.

Despite my gloved hand protecting my face, my cheeks ached from the cold. My fingers and toes were numb as I trudged forward. During the hours of my drive, I'd seen only a half dozen other vehicles, and yet as I moved forward, that was what I yearned to see.

The snow glistened as I imagined white light dancing on the newly fallen accumulation.

Looking back, I hoped to see a car, a truck, or maybe a snowplow.

I'd read about igloos. The thought came and went as I imagined digging into the growing drifts. It still seemed as if it would be cold, but at least I'd be out of the wind.

The howl of the blowing wind played tricks as I searched again for a vehicle.

Nothing.

Time lost meaning as my thoughts went to my parents. I couldn't imagine their disappointment at my behavior, at leaving the city before the holiday and two weeks before my wedding. And yet I loved them and I knew they loved me. We would work this out...unless I never returned.

I spun again at the sound of something over the howling wind.

Do mirages only appear in deserts?

Two headlights pierced the snow-filled darkness, growing bigger and brighter.

Is this real?

My heart beat faster, my circulation returning and delivering pain to my extremities.

Tears threatened to freeze on my cheeks as through the darkness, a black snow-covered truck appeared.

Waving my arms with what little energy remained, I felt my knees give out as the truck came to a stop, and I fell to the snow. A face appeared before me. The air filled with small vapors as a man spoke.

"Jesus, lady, are you all right?"

Piercing green eyes stared down at me from below a bright orange hat and above a heavy brown coat.

"Cold." It was all I could articulate with my frozen lips.

"Fuck," the man muttered as he reached for my hand.

"Ouch," I called out as pain radiated from my fingers.

The man's head shook as he reached beneath me. "Can you lift your arms?" His deep voice rumbled through my freezing mind, cracking the ice and infiltrating it with warmth.

I wasn't sure if I answered, nodded, or spoke. My concentration was on doing as he asked and lifting my arms around his neck. Strong arms lifted me from the snow and pulled me toward his coat-covered chest. I tucked my cheek against him. As I inhaled against the warm material, the scent of a campfire such as those from real wood filled my senses.

"What are you doing out here?"

My teeth chattered as I tried to speak.

Holding me with one arm, he opened the door to his truck and placed me on the seat. "I'm going to get you someplace warm."

Strapping the seatbelt over me, he inclined the seat. Marvelous warmth blew from the vents as I closed my eyes. The scent of burning wood brought back a happier time. I remembered sitting by the hearth in my grandparents' cottage. It was on a lake with a real wood-burning fireplace.

I fought to keep my eyes open. After all, this man was a stranger. My battle was in vain. With my energy depleted, the warmer world faded to unconsciousness.

* * *

I snuggled against the softness of the warm blanket moments before my eyelids fluttered open.

Before me was a raging fire, flames leaping as damp logs snapped and crackled. The fireplace was made of sandstone, much like the one at my grand-parents'.

Panic bubbled within me at the prospect that maybe this was heaven, a place of comfort in my memory. Maybe there weren't clouds, harps, streets of gold, and pearly gates. Instead, the afterlife was one of comfort. My stomach twisted in hunger.

I shouldn't be hungry in heaven.

Raking my fingers through my disheveled hair, I began to look around. The only illumination was from the fire and a small kerosene lamp sitting on a table. Sitting up, I wrapped the quilt tighter around me. Out of the corner of my eye, I noticed my clothes lying over the footboard of the bed, stretched out to dry. Peeking under the quilt, I confirmed that I was only wearing my bra and panties.

Wiggling my fingers and toes, I could feel them ache. The skin was red. My cheeks felt sunburnt, and my hair was unkempt.

Quickly, I turned from side to side, wondering who I'd see, who was with me, and who took off my clothes.

The cabin where I found myself was rustic like my grandparents' place but smaller.

"Hello?" I called.

The only answer came from the fire's sounds and the wind beyond the cabin walls. Through the windows the night sky was still filled with falling snow. It wasn't difficult to tell that I was alone. There was nowhere to hide in one room.

Faint memories of a man came to mind. Green eyes, an orange hat, and a deep voice.

With my feet bare yet warmed, I stood; the after-effects of the cold sent pins and needles to the soles. Tentatively, I walked around, admiring the quaintness of the furnishings. In the warm firelight, I ran my hand over each piece. Most appeared handmade, a table and two chairs, a bed with a wooden head- and footboard, and a wooden sofa with long cushions.

Near the bed was a table with an old-fashioned pitcher and washbasin. Above the old china set was a cloudy oval mirror. The reflection in it wasn't of the heir to Wade Pharmaceutical or the future Mrs. Butler.

My long blond hair was wavy from the snow and drying by the fire. Any makeup I'd applied was gone, yet Mother Nature had left her mark. My cheeks and lips were pink. I ran my tongue over the bottom lip and then the top, bringing a bit of moisture.

A quick check confirmed that my clothes were still too wet to be worn.

The kitchen area, separated by the small table, consisted of a sink with an old pump, the kind that needed priming, a counter, some shelves, cupboards, and a stove that also used wood as fuel to create heat. Upon the two metal burners were an old coffeepot and a pan filled with water.

I turned off the burner under the water as it was beginning to boil. Using a small towel, I held onto the coffeepot's handle and lifted, pleased to find it heavy. Dark drops percolated within the glass top on the lid as the aroma of coffee joined the scent of the fire.

While coffee would be good, my empty stomach hoped for more. I opened a cupboard to find a few cans of soup. By the way it looked beyond the windows, sending for Uber Eats was out of the question. That thought led me to thoughts of my phone. I found it on the table near the bed, without any signal and with a very low battery.

There was nothing to suggest this cabin had electricity. Charging my phone or anything else was out of the question.

The cool cement floor beneath my feet was covered with an array of rugs of all sizes. The wood walls gave the feel of a real log cabin. The farther I moved away from the fireplace, the cooler the air became.

It was as I settled back on the thick blanket where I'd awakened and wrapped the quilt around me that the door to my side opened wide. A gust of cold wind filled with snow preceded the man from my memory. His arms were filled with logs. After giving me a quick glance, he kicked the door closed with his long leg. When he stood erect, he was tall, taller than me.

I obviously didn't know this man or anything about him other than he'd saved my life and apparently disrobed me, yet without a word, my pulse increased and my cheeks felt flush.

His green eyes came my way before setting the logs in a round holder near the fireplace. Wiping his gloved hands one over the other, he dusted the snow, bark, and dirt to the floor. One by one, he pulled the gloves away from his long fingers, and still his gaze stayed glued on me.

I tugged on the quilt, suddenly reminded that this had been the man who removed my clothes. By looking at him, it was impossible to judge his age in the firelight. He wasn't old or young and yet something about him held my attention.

The ends of his lips twitched, perhaps humored by my unease.

Unzipping the front of his brown coat, he shrugged it off, shaking the snow to the floor. Next, he removed his stocking cap, revealing a crown of messy dark hair. Finally breaking his stare, he turned to hang the coat and his stocking cap upon a peg near the door. The shirt under it was flannel and unbuttoned over a thermal shirt beneath.

Survival 101 came to mind with his layering.

Without glancing at my clothes, I knew I'd failed that test.

I worked my way to my feet and when he turned back, I spoke, "Thank you."

He lifted his chin. "Not exactly a good night for a walk." His gaze went to the window as white swirled in the darkness. "Of course, you're welcome to leave if you want."

I shook my head. "I don't want that, not now."

Nodding, the man walked to the stove and pulled two metal mugs from a shelf. Without asking, he filled both with hot coffee and brought one to me.

His lips curled into a smile as he scanned the quilt and handed me the mug. "I usually try to introduce myself before I take off a lady's clothes."

"Usually?"

He nodded. "Usually. As with any rule, there are exceptions."

I placed the mug of coffee on the hearth and extended my hand. "Thank you for saving me. I'm Julia."

The flames reflected in his eyes like glowing embers. As I stepped closer, the aroma of the outdoors surrounded us, fresh and cool. Although he'd been outside, as his fingers encased my hand, his touch wasn't cold. It was the opposite, as if there was energy within him flowing from him to me. Our connection was a jolt like I had never before experienced. It shot through me, electrifying my skin and sending sparks to my insides.

Pulling my hand away, I stared down at it, wondering if he'd felt the same thing.

What is it?

Maybe it was from the near frostbite.

As I lifted my chin, he began to speak. "Are you sure?"

"Am I sure?"

"Julia, perhaps you should reconsider your gratitude." He looked around. "You're in a remote cabin in a blizzard in northern Wisconsin without a way to contact civilization. Does that sound like you were saved?" Small lines formed around his vibrant green eyes as he grinned. "Or are you perhaps captured?"

Chapter 03

Julia

My mouth felt suddenly dry as color drained from my cheeks. I feigned a laugh. "I believe saved. You see, I would have frozen to death without your help."

Amusement danced in his gaze along with the reflection of the fire. "Julia, I'm Van. I suppose now that we know one another's names, taking off our clothes is acceptable." He tugged on the sleeves of his flannel shirt and pulled it off, tossing it onto the sofa's cushions. Without the flannel, a light gray thermal shirt remained, nicely stretched across his wide shoulders and chest.

Sitting on the blanket, I said, "I believe I'm down to as few clothes as possible."

Van shook his head as he picked up his mug of coffee. "I know for a fact that's not true."

Technically, he was right. I was still wearing my bra and panties.

I reached for the mug I'd set on the hearth and

wrapped my fingers around the warm metal. "How long do you think it will be until we can leave?"

"If that was your car I saw down the road, I think you may need to consider a tow truck after the spring thaw."

"What?"

"In all honesty, we'll need some melting to find it. It was mostly buried." He took a sip of his coffee. "I'm glad I saw it. That's why I started looking for the driver."

A deep sigh left my lips. "It's a rental car. I can't tell the rental company I lost their car in a snowbank."

Van scoffed. "You could tell them you ran it off the road, but the good news is you didn't hit a tree."

My mind went back to the car. "All of my things are in the trunk. I even left my purse in there." I tilted my head toward the bed. "All I took with me was my phone."

He nodded. "That would be why I couldn't find anything to identify you." He tilted his chin toward the phone. "That's not going to do you much good here. Once the snow stops, you may be able to go up the hill and get a signal. I recommend you save whatever battery you have."

My shoulders slumped as I shook my head. "It figures."

"And what is that, Julia?"

"I finally decide to do something for myself and look at me." My lips came together.

The tips of his lips curled upward as his green gaze scanned me. "I'm looking."

Setting down the coffee mug, I stood again, pulling the quilt tightly around me and took a step toward the small table and kerosene lamp. A million things swirled in my head, not unlike the snow beyond the window. I didn't know Van. That meant that I could keep quiet or maybe take the opportunity to vent. I decided on somewhere in between. "My whole life has been planned by others, and the one time I decide to take charge of it, I mess that up." I pulled out one of the chairs from the table and sat. As I did, I ran my hand over the table's surface. "Do you live here?" I asked, hoping to change the subject.

"No."

My chin snapped up. "Who does?"

"No one, to my knowledge."

"Are we trespassing?"

"This cabin is used during hunting season. I thought, given the weather, that it would be empty. With as cold as you were, I didn't want to risk trying to get into town and also driving off the road."

"Are you from around here?"

Van nodded. "But you're not."

"No," I said with a sigh. "I thought I could..." My head shook. "It doesn't matter."

Van reached for my coffee and brought it to me, placing it on the table. "Are you hungry?"

"Famished." I looked around. "Is there...food besides the old cans of soup?"

He scoffed. "I see you've searched."

"There isn't much to search."

"The good news is that I have a case of nectarines in my truck. And yes, there is always the soup." He nodded toward a cupboard under the counter. "I'm not sure how old the cans are. We could search for expiration dates. There's a pan to warm it if we want."

That reminded me of the pot of water on the stove. "I turned the water off, it was boiling."

Van nodded as he went to the pan and poured the water into a large jar. "This is to drink. I'm not sure about the water out of the pump. Boiling it first is best."

It felt as though I was secluded with one of those mountain men from the movies.

"Why do you have nectarines in your truck?" I asked.

"I like nectarines."

It was my turn to smile. "So you keep a case in your truck, just in case?"

"I order them by the case, and I'd recently picked

up a shipment from the post office in town. At this moment, I'm glad I forgot to take them into my house."

"Me too."

Van headed toward the door, and stopped, picking up his flannel shirt from where he'd dropped it on the sofa. "You're welcome to keep wearing the quilt, but I would guess that this shirt would make a decent-length dress." He brought it to me. "Your choice, but your clothes are still cold and wet."

I reached out and took the shirt. "Thank you."

"There isn't a lot of privacy here. If you want to put it on, I'll be outside for a minute getting our dinner."

Another thought came to me. "What about a bathroom?"

"There's an outhouse about twenty yards from the door."

For only a moment, my mouth dropped open. "You're not serious."

He grinned. "As a matter of fact, I am. I even shoveled a path out to it when I went for more wood. And the increased accumulation of snow works like insulation. Once you're inside, the wind won't freeze you."

"The wind doesn't need to—the cold will."

"Not if you hurry."

My head shook. "This is just unbelievable."

Van went to a skinny cupboard near the table with the old pitcher and basin. Opening it, he pulled out a pair of what appeared to be rubber pants, complete with boots and suspenders. "After you put my shirt on, you can wear these out to the outhouse."

My eyes narrowed. "What are those?"

"Waders," he replied as if I should have known the answer.

"Waders? Aren't those for fishing?"

"Very good."

"You said the cabin is used for hunting."

"During the summer, it's used to hunt fish," Van said with a grin. "Instead of a gun, a fishing pole is used. There's a large lake nearby."

"Nectarines." I reminded.

Leaving the waders on the bed, Van put his coat back on, his orange hat, and his gloves. When he turned my way, he winked. "I don't think I've ever looked more forward to seeing that old shirt."

His gaze lingered a bit longer than it should've before he turned and disappeared beyond the door, leaving a powdering of snow on the floor in his wake.

Despite the gust of cold air, Van's comment warmed me from my head to my toes.

How was it that this man I barely knew could incite that visceral response with a relatively benign comment about clothing and the man I was engaged to couldn't or didn't make me feel that way even when he was kissing and touching me?

I refused to give that any more thought.

Besides, I wasn't engaged.

Not anymore.

Lifting my left hand, I stared at my bare ring finger.

The last time I saw the huge four-carat diamond, it was on the counter next to Skylar's phone and a note:

Beth needs you. Goodbye, Julia.

Of course, since I left, Skylar has tried to call and text. I haven't answered.

Taking one last look at the closed door, I dropped the quilt. As I reached for Van's flannel shirt, the tempered air sent goose bumps over my skin and caused my nipples to tighten beneath my bra. Without thinking, I brought the soft material to my nose, closed my eyes, and inhaled.

The fresh scent of soap, the aroma of fire, and the spice of cologne all created an enticing concoction that even in this short time had me thinking of Van. Slipping my arms into the sleeves, I realized that Van had been right; this could be a dress. As I began to button the front, the tails in the front and back came to just above my knees.

While I had dresses that were shorter, wearing this man's shirt—a man whom I barely knew—somehow felt more scandalous. I was in the process of rolling the sleeves up when the door opened. As he'd done before, Van used his booted foot to kick the door closed. This time, instead of logs, his arms were filled with a wooden crate that he set down on the floor. Between the slats of wood, the orange spheres made my mouth water.

After shedding the hat, gloves, and coat, Van retrieved the crate from the floor and brought it to the kitchen counter. Once there, he turned in my direction and smiled. Without a word, his green stare scanned me from my messy hair to my bare toes.

With each passing second, I became more self-conscious, and yet he didn't speak. Van's lips formed a straight line, his cheeks rose, and his eyes sparkled with flecks of gold I was just now noticing.

"Thanks for the shirt," I said, slapping my thighs with the palms of my hands. "It's better than wearing that quilt."

"It definitely is."

His deeper tenor and slower cadence twisted my core and returned my nipples to their hardened state from the earlier cool air.

"You're making me self-conscious. What are you thinking?"

Van walked around me, all the way around, the entire time keeping his eyes on me. "I think it's better if I don't say."

"What?"

His smile grew. "I'm thinking that if I ever plan an abduction in the middle of a blizzard, I need to remember a flannel shirt because on you, it's sexy as hell."

I lifted my hands to my cheeks, feeling the growing heat.

Van took a step toward me. "Come on, Julia, there has to be a man in your life who tells you how damn sexy you are."

Swallowing, I turned away, avoiding the subject, and began to open the crate of nectarines.

As I tugged on a plastic cord holding the lid in place, Van's hand came over mine.

The electricity from before returned.

When I looked up, Van held a pocket knife in his other hand. "Step back so you don't get cut."

Without speaking, I did as he said. The plastic snapped as the blade sliced through it. The muscles in his arms bulged as he lifted the lid and placed it under the counter. Turning, he held out a nectarine. "Dinner."

I took the golden and red fruit from him, careful that we didn't touch again. "Thank you."

Retrieving our mugs, I added more coffee to each one and took them to the hearth. Even with the roaring fire, the air farther away was chilled. Basking in the warmth, I settled on the blankets and rugs where I'd awakened. After taking off his boots and leaving them by the door, Van joined me on the blanket.

With our legs crossed, we both stared into the flames. Every once in a while, our knees would touch as we both ate our nectarines and drank our coffee. As the fire warmed me outside, the coffee and his incidental touches warmed me inside.

Chapter 04

Julia

My teeth chattered as I opened the door to the outhouse and sheepishly smiled up at Van. The snow blew around us as he tucked me under his arm, and we hurried back to the cabin. Once inside, I shivered as I shrugged off my down-filled coat and looked down at the ridiculous waders.

"Thank you for going out there with me."

"What good is it to hold a beautiful woman captive if I let her freeze to death?"

"Or if she's eaten by wolves." I had been ready to venture outside to the outhouse by myself until I heard the howl of a wolf. There weren't many literal wolves to deal with in the Chicago suburbs.

"Wolf attacks are rare," Van said with a grin.

"Rare implies that they do occur." Holding onto the wall, I pushed down the giant rubber waders until I could step out with one foot and then the other. When I turned, Van was looking in my direction. "If you say the waders looked sexy, I'll know you're lying."

He came toward me and grabbed the waders, taking them to the pegs on the wall to let them dry. "No, Julia, the waders aren't sexy."

I nodded. "Maybe you don't lie like other men."

My attention went to the one bed. I reached for a pillow. "I can sleep by the fire."

"There are plenty of blankets on the bed. You'll be warm."

"How do you know?" I asked, pulling back layer after layer of blanket. "You're right."

Van gestured out to the room. "I figured if all these blankets are out here, there would be plenty on the bed."

"Shit," I said, noticing my phone. Picking it up, I saw that not only was there no signal, the battery was down to less than ten percent. "I meant to turn this off." Once I did, I put it back on the bedside table. Slowly, I turned toward Van. His dark hair was mussed from the hat and there was dark stubble on his cheeks. His coat and boots were again near the door. Starting at the floor, I scanned his wool socks, long legs in faded denim, the way his shirt stretched over his chest and arms, his five o'clock shadow, high cheekbones, emerald green eyes, and back to his messy dark hair.

It wasn't until my scan reached his stare that I

realized Van had been doing the same to me. Nervously, I ran my fingers through my hair and laughed. Seeing the door, I asked, "Should we lock that?"

"If anyone finds their way out here, they deserve a warm shelter."

"But what if they're bad people?"

"What if I told you that I was a bad person?"

I reached again for the pillow and hugged it in front of me. "I wouldn't believe you."

Van took a step toward me. "Why?"

I stepped back as I hugged the pillow tighter. "Because you saved me. You gave me coffee and fed me." I grinned. "And protected me from the wolves."

He came even closer, his scent clouding my thoughts as he reached toward me and then...beyond me, pulling down the blankets on the bed. "Climb in, Julia. You'll be warm in no time, and I promise it's more comfortable than the floor." He lifted his chin toward the fireplace. "I'll sleep by the fire and keep it going so we don't freeze."

Bending my knee, I knelt on the soft mattress and wiggled my way under the blankets. Once I did, Van pulled them up over me. For a moment he hesitated. Shaking his head, he turned, but before he could go, I seized his large hand.

"Wait."

Turning his hand over, I ran my fingers over his palm. "Your hands, they're not callous."

"I have a great lotion regimen."

A smile came to my lips. "I was beginning to think you lied about not living here. But if you lived out here and chopped wood, your hands would be rougher."

He shook his head. "Don't try to figure me out."

"Is that mutual? Are you not trying to figure me out?"

Sitting on the edge of the bed, he sucked in a breath. "I already have you figured out."

"Am I that obvious?"

"Somewhere there's a man who did you wrong. You're searching for a life that isn't planned out, and in the process, you found yourself stranded in a snowstorm."

"I wasn't completely stranded," I said. "I followed the white ribbon."

Van's gaze narrowed. "The white ribbon."

"With all the snow, I couldn't see the road, so I told myself to follow the white ribbon."

He nodded. "What did he do?"

Pressing my lips together, I shook my head.

"I don't say this often, but I'm sorry he hurt you." Van's finger traced down my cheek in a display of familiarity that felt surprisingly right. "I hope you find what you're looking for."

"I'm not sure what I'm looking for. I think it was to get away."

His smile bloomed. "If that was it, I'd say you got it."

"I did." When he started to stand, I again reached for his hand. "I just ended a...relationship, and I'm not looking for a new one."

"That's good because I'm not the relationship kind."

"You're the good kind, though. You didn't need to rescue me or take care of me, but you did."

"Julia, I promise, I'm not good."

I fought the tears as I held tight to his hand. "I'm tired of pretending to be happy and pretending that everything is the way it should be. I thought maybe I could get away and find myself." My gaze went to his eyes. Letting go of his hand, I reached up to palm his cheek. "I found you instead."

"I think, technically, I found you."

I scooted over to the cold side of the bed. "You can sleep here. Maybe tomorrow the snow will have stopped."

Van shook his head. "You don't know what you're doing."

"I do."

"Listen, I'm not against a one-night stand. It's that you're not the kind of woman I would want a one-night stand with."

"Oh," I said, turning away.

"Shit." Van reached for my chin and turned it back. "That was a fucking compliment. I'm the damn wolf you heard out there. It's who I am in my private life and in my career. You are Little Red Riding Hood, and the last thing you should do is invite the wolf into your bed."

"Weeks before my wedding, I found out my best friend is pregnant and the man I was engaged to is the father."

"Fuck."

I nodded. "I'll sleep over here. I'm not asking you to make love to me. I'm offering half the bed."

"I don't work that way," Van said as he walked away.

My eyes closed as I tried to make sense of anything that had happened over the last forty-eight hours. The stress and cold had worn me down. I opened my eyes to see Van crouched near the fireplace, tending to the fire inside. His words made me wonder about him.

What kind of private life does he have?

What does he do in business that he considers himself a wolf?

I was almost asleep when I heard the wind as the door opened. When I looked up, the kerosene lamp on the table was extinguished and Van was gone.

He probably went to the outhouse, I told myself.

Time passed.

Uncertain of where he could have gone or if he'd leave me alone, I sat up against the hand-carved headboard and pulled the blankets over me. The fire snapped and crackled. The wind outside continued to blow. I reached for my phone to see the time, and then, remembering it was turned off, I set it back on the bedside stand. My eyelids grew heavy, but I refused to lie back.

Finally, to my relief, the door opened. Through the firelight, I watched as Van took off his hat, gloves, coat, and boots. My lip disappeared behind my teeth as he unbuckled his belt, unfastened his blue jeans, and allowed them to fall to his ankles. His silk boxer briefs weren't those of a mountain man. They showed each bulge and pulled tight over his muscular behind. Reaching over his head, he tugged on the back of his thermal shirt and pulled it over his head, revealing his wide chest with just the right amount of dark hair.

Inconspicuously, I moved lower under the blankets so as to not alert him that I was still awake.

The moving of the blankets and leaning of the mattress caused my eyes to open. "Van?"

"You'll regret this, Julia."

Chapter 05

Julia

Van slid under the blankets until he radiated warmth beside me. The twisting in my core at watching him disrobe turned painful as he turned to me, our noses nearly touching. His large hand gently came to my cheek as he pulled me closer until our lips met.

His approach firm and strong, there was nothing tentative in it. Van tasted like coffee and nectarines as his tongue teased my lips, and I willingly allowed him entrance. Moans and whimpers echoed throughout the cabin as his touch skirted under the long flannel shirt, freeing my breasts from my bra and taunting my nipples.

His green eyes blazed with the power of a raging forest fire as he stared down at me. "Take off my shirt."

It wasn't a request. It wasn't even disguised as a request. Van's tone left no room for argument as my fingers hurried with the buttons, one by one until the final one was freed.

Van pulled back the blankets as I freed my arms. With a quick move behind my back, he released the clasp on my bra, and without a word he removed it, sending it somewhere to the floor.

His breathing deepened as he stared. "It took every fucking ounce of restraint to not do that when I undressed you, and now, you're even more gorgeous than I imagined." He leaned down, sucking one nipple and then the other. As soon as his warm lips would disappear, the cool air would attack.

Blood rushed to my breasts, making them heavy as his five o'clock shadow abraded my skin.

"Van." I couldn't articulate any further.

His finger came to my lips. "You invited me, Julia. The rest is up to me." Fire crackled in his stare. "That's my rule. Can you follow rules?"

The answer was that I could, I had all my life, but at this moment, it felt like the opposite, as if I was breaking free.

"Julia."

I nodded against his finger. Opening my lips, I took it in my mouth and sucked.

"Fuck," he growled. His head dipped as he kissed lower, down my ribs, my stomach, and to the waist-line of my panties.

No longer was I stranded in a blizzard. I was lost

in a cloud of wanton lust unlike any I'd experienced before. My mind was incapable of thinking beyond the bed, beyond Van, and beyond the assault on my sensory system. This must be what it was like to be with a man who knew how to please a woman and did so without fanfare. Van's touch was commanding yet enticing.

I couldn't keep track of the ministrations of his lips or hands. Like a sculptor, he molded me to his liking, bringing me more pleasure than I knew existed.

Whatever Van was doing, I wanted more.

If I was asked when my panties disappeared, I wouldn't be able to answer. If I was questioned on when his boxer briefs vanished, I'd be at an equal loss.

My fingernails threatened the cotton sheets as he moved lower, nipping, licking, and lapping my core. My back arched and my knees squeezed as Van brought me to an orgasm unlike any I'd ever experienced.

As I worked to catch my breath, Van's green eyes appeared before me. "You said you didn't invite me to this bed to make love."

I nodded. "I didn't."

"I don't want to make love, Julia. I'm so fucking hard; I want to fuck you like you've never been fucked."

"I never have."

His entire body stiffened. "What did you say?"

"Please." I held tight to his shoulders. "I've done...this...up to...but we stopped." His eyes closed. "Van, I know I may never see you again. Hell, I don't even know your last name, but I saved myself for someone who didn't deserve me and look where it got me. I want this. Please, fuck me."

His head shook. "You really don't know what you're asking for."

I reached my hand lower, finding his hard cock. Wrapping my fingers around him as best as I could, I ran my hand up and down. "I do."

With his body between my bent legs, Van pushed up on his hands on either side of me. My heart beat in triple time as he stared down at me. "I want to take you."

"Do it."

"I'll hurt you and that won't stop me."

I wiggled my hips. "I've been hurt, Van. This is physical and I promise I can take it."

There were things I'd built up in my head. I made them out to be better or worse than they were. The Eiffel Tower was smaller than I imagined. The British crown jewels were more spectacular than I anticipated. Sex was always right outside my reality. I'd heard other women talk, and I'd read books. As Van and I came together as one, the union was both worse and better.

I cried out, unable to stifle my scream as Van took what I'd saved for someone else.

Even though he said my pain wouldn't stop him, it did. He stilled and brought his nose to mine. "I promise it will get better."

Swallowing, I nodded. "I believe you."

The worst was over as the better grew.

Like a volcano, the heat within me increased. Van didn't only satisfy my core, filling me completely, he also tended to the rest of me, and his touch was everywhere. Synapses fired and nerve endings responded. Never had I been so alive or so lavished with attention.

The ecstasy didn't end with my next orgasm or even his.

Throughout the night one of us would wake and it would begin again.

I wasn't certain when it occurred to me that we hadn't used protection. As soon as it did, I justified that I was on birth control—after all, I was to be on my honeymoon in two weeks. While I hoped Van was clean, I couldn't ignore the way he felt inside me, his skin against mine, and our bodies united.

Finally, sleep won.

When I awoke, light seeped through the windows and the bed at my side was cool. Moving, I felt tenderness where I never before had been tender. As memories came back of everything we'd done the night before, a smile came to my lips.

Sitting up, I saw Van near the fireplace, teasing the embers. He was fully dressed as he'd been before coming to bed.

"Good morning," I said sheepishly.

"I let the fire go out. I should have it going soon." He turned my way. "Stay under the covers. It's probably forty degrees or less out here."

I wiggled my nose, realizing it was cold. "After you get the fire going, you could join me."

Van remained quiet, his concentration on his job as fire master.

I saw the glow radiate against his skin at the same time the logs began to snap.

Van stood tall and walked toward me. "Julia, if things were different... If *I* were different, I would want a woman like you in my life. I'm not different. I told you that you'd regret last night, and I am sure you do."

My head shook. "I don't." Keeping the blankets up to my shoulders, I sat against the headboard. "Van, I'm not some damsel in distress." I giggled, thinking that was exactly who I was. "Not usually. I'm not looking for a man to save me. I don't regret last night. I'll carry it with me forever. You made me feel desired and..." I searched for the words. "Good." That simple word was the perfect description. "I felt good and real, the way it feels to not pretend. It felt amazing. I don't need to know your last name or you mine. I'm on the pill. We don't owe one another anything. This was two people stranded along the white ribbon."

Van took a deep breath. "The snow has stopped. I was going to walk out to the road. If it's plowed, I think we can get you into town. As for your car—"

I waved him off. "Town is good. Ashland, right?"

"Yes, that's the closest town with resources you'll need." He came closer.

"Good. I have reservations at a hotel there. I'll deal with my car later. You, Van no-last-name, have done your part in rescuing this damsel." I reached for his hand. "I regret nothing. I hope you don't."

His Adam's apple bobbed. "I have regrets, but last night isn't one of them. My regret is that I'm not someone else."

My cheeks rose. "I like who you are."

"You don't know who I am." Walking to the end of the bed, he lifted my clothes from the footboard. "Your clothes are dry."

"Then I guess I'm done wearing your shirt."

"I'll never look at that shirt the same way."

"You don't owe me any promises," I said as I pulled back the covers. Turning to Van, I asked, "Have you seen my panties?"

Chapter 06

Julia
A FEW DAYS LATER

"*M*iss McGrath?" the older gentleman asked, standing to shake my hand.

I reached forward and shook Mr. Fields's hand. "Thank you for seeing me today."

"I was surprised you were able to get here so soon. We've had some difficult weather."

Warmth filled my cheeks as I recalled the difficult weather. "Yes, I had a problem with my rental car. Thankfully, Chase at the automotive shop was able to rescue it and all of my belongings."

I was currently dressed for success. With a silk blouse, high-waisted black slacks, and high-heeled black boots, I wasn't left to interview in a shirt owned by a man with only a first name. Yet as I stood in the office of Fields and Smith, I knew that the white ribbon had taken me to a place that not only rescued me from the cold but also showed me that I could survive without Skylar or life's well-laid plans.

"You're wrong, Van. I don't regret a thing." That was my thought as I waited for my interview.

I deleted the numerous text messages from Skylar from my now fully charged phone. I'd spoken to my mother. She was caught somewhere between supporting my decision and not. "There's more than love involved here," she told me more than once.

She was right. There was also fidelity and trust.

I'd also spoken to my friend Vicki. She was supposed to be my bridesmaid. Vicki, Beth, and I had been close since high school. Vicki was shocked to hear my news. "I swear, if I knew, I'd have told you," she'd said.

I wanted to believe her, unwilling to lose both of my best friends to Skylar's infidelity.

Over the past few days, I'd also gotten a feel for the beautiful Great Lake shore town. Ashland was a city with a small-town feel. Despite the snowfall, the streets and sidewalks were cleared, allowing residents and visitors to walk about. From my hotel, I found the cafes, restaurants, and stores inviting and the people welcoming. Many of the downtown buildings had some of the prettiest murals I'd ever seen.

Mr. Fields appeared. "Miss McGrath, Mr. Sherman will see you now."

"Is he your client?" I asked.

"Yes, ma'am, Donovan Sherman is a private man. He'll have the only voice in your hiring. Please don't take it personally if he decides against it. As I said, he's private and particular."

"He wanted to see me?"

"Yes. I can't promise you more than that."

As I walked down the hallway toward the conference room a step behind Mr. Fields, I decided private would be nice. If I got the job offer, I liked the idea of having time to myself.

Mr. Fields opened the door.

The man within, younger than the old man I anticipated, was turned toward the window. His attire was what I'd expected, an expensive suit all the way to the cuff links and Italian loafers. His shoulders were broad and the suit was custom, accentuating his toned torso and trim waist. It was as he turned that I sucked in a breath, the blood drained from my face, and my knees felt weak.

"Mr. Fields," Van said, his green gaze fixed on me, "thank you. I'll let you know if we need you."

"Mr. Sherman, I'm willing to stay and—"

Van interrupted, "That won't be necessary."

As Van spoke, the fire from the cabin ignited in his eyes.

Once Mr. Fields was gone, Van came closer. "Am I to think this was all coincidental?"

"You said your name was Van."

"Donovan. Van is shortened."

Honestly, Mr. Fields had never told me his

client's name. Shaking my head, I turned to leave. "I'm sorry, Mr. Sherman, this isn't what I was..."

He reached for my hand. "When I saw the name Julia on the schedule and read your résumé, I had to know if it was you."

My hand tingled in his with the electricity of our first touch.

"I-I...I'm not looking for anything except a job to take me away from my life."

"Write my story, Julia. Once you learn about the real me, you'll be able to see me for the wolf I warned you I am."

"You want me to stay?"

"You realize the job description includes living on my estate."

A smile crept across my lips. "Estate? It's one room."

"No. That was a cabin on the outskirts of my property. You'll have your own suite."

"Isn't that generous?"

His green eyes shimmered. "At first."

Van opened a briefcase on the table and removed something small, holding it in his hand. "I got this object on the far-fetched chance that Julia McGrath was Julia no-last-name."

"What is it?"

"Will you take the job?"

"I don't need the money," I said. "I want you to know that."

Van's head tilted. "Before you answer, I have an even more enticing proposition."

My pulse increased. "I'm only looking for a job."

"I told you that I'm a wolf in business. I take opportunities when they present themselves."

I shook my head. "I just walked away from a relationship that involved business."

"And Skylar Butler fucked your best friend."

I sucked in a breath. "How do you know that?"

"You told me."

"I never told you his name."

Van's jaw clenched. "Do you want to fuck him back?"

I took a step away and walked toward the window, looking out on snow-blanketed Ashland and a frozen Chequamegon Bay. The snow globe had settled over a quaint community. "I told you, we never—"

Van was behind me, his warmth on my back and his breath at my collarbone sending chills over my skin. "Figuratively, Julia. I have the answer. Marry me."

I spun around until my breasts were against his strong, solid chest. Tilting my chin upward, I asked, "What?"

"It can be in name only. You'll live with me. Sex will be...discussed. I made some inquiries and called in a few favors. As of this morning, I own twenty-one percent of the shares of Wade. Marry me and send Skylar and Marlin Butler into bankruptcy or at least out of Wade Pharmaceutical."

"I don't know how you know this. Did you save me for this reason?"

He laughed. "I had no idea who you were, just as you didn't know who I was." He lifted my left hand. "I'm well aware that you don't need money, but you do need controlling interest in your family's company. Without that controlling interest, you'll need money. Your father's paranoia is justified, the threat just not coming from the direction he believes. Marlin Butler has been in negotiations with two large pharmaceutical companies. He has plans for Wade. He's been biding his time, waiting for his son to marry you to make himself very wealthy at the expense of your family's company."

I couldn't believe what Van was saying and at the same time, I did. I imagined a grand scheme orchestrated by Marlin Butler. I knew deep down that the man who claimed to be my father's best friend was capable of what Van suggested.

Does Skylar know? Is he part of the plan or an unknowing pawn like myself?

"Marry me, Julia. You don't need the money, but together we'll secure controlling interest in Wade

Pharmaceutical, and as a bonus, I'll enjoy watching the Butlers squirm."

"Van, I...I don't know you."

"You know what it's like to have me inside you." His voice dropped an octave, twisting my core. "You yourself said you and Butler never went that far. You were going to marry a man you didn't really know, one who fucked your best friend. Marry one who you know can satisfy you."

Still holding my left hand, Van turned mine palm up and laid something light in my grasp. When his hand moved, I saw it. A white ribbon.

"Say yes. Say the white ribbon brought us together."

My heart beat against my breastbone as I stared down at the coiled ribbon in my hand. When I looked up, his emerald stare was on me.

"Come, Miss McGrath, I require an answer."

"If I say yes, is that my invitation to you?"

"Are you asking if the rest is up to me, if from now on I'm in control?"

I nodded, remembering what he'd said as he joined me in the bed.

"Do you regret following that rule in the cabin?"

"No, but even you said that rules have exceptions."

"Not that one. My rule hasn't changed." He grinned. "That doesn't mean I won't enjoy your plays for power. Let's see where this ribbon leads. Marry me."

"Will I regret it?" I asked, recalling Van's warning from before.

"Maybe." When I didn't respond, he added, "Less than you'd regret marrying Butler." His eyebrows rose. "Your answer?"

It was the most insane thing I'd ever contemplated doing, and I'd contemplated more than a few less-than-sane things over my twenty-four years.

Seeing Van with my smaller hand in his, for the first time, I felt the flutter that was supposed to accompany this question. With his intense gaze shining down on me, it was only the two of us as it had been in that cabin. There was no large hall filled with people and no big presentation. My answer wouldn't incite cheers and applause. No one would hear it except the man who proposed.

There wasn't even a ring, only a white ribbon.

I closed my fingers around the ribbon. "Yes, Van, I'll marry you."

Chapter 07

Julia

*V*an's intense green gaze penetrated my thoughts, his spicy cologne tingled my senses, and his proximity sent energy through my circulation. I was on sensory overload as I stared down at the white ribbon, closed it within my fist, and closed my eyes. I turned toward the coolness of the window as the magnitude of the answer I'd given to Van settled within me much as a weight dragging me beneath the ice and into the depths of Lake Superior.

I'd only days earlier freed myself from a marriage commitment.

Despite Van's presence, thoughts of Skylar and all that we'd planned ran circles in my mind, clouding my ability to think rationally. Beginning with our childhood, the memories of Skylar and me fast-forwarded to a few days ago. Never had our future been in question. Until it was.

Do I love him?

I thought I had, but never ever was I *in love* with Skylar. That revelation gave me strength to move forward.

Have I ever been in love?

Maybe Beth was. Maybe she was in love with Skylar and he with her. That thought brought on an epiphany—I didn't care. I didn't care if Skylar loved Beth or vice versa. Maybe I was simply numb. The anger and hurt that I felt reading Beth's text message had faded into the blinding snowstorm. The greatest emotion I felt to thoughts related to the end of my engagement was relief.

Van was near. I felt the warmth of him on my back. Without touching me, he sent energy from him to me. I spun in place, my sight coming to his wide chest. Looking up, I swallowed and spoke, "I've spent my life following other people's plans."

"Are you rescinding your answer?"

I nodded. "I am. This is too fast. I don't know what I was thinking. Perhaps I wasn't. I need time to be me."

His large hands came to my shoulders. Though I felt his power, his touch was gentle and reassuring. His tone and tenor ricocheted through my body. "You can be you, Julia. From the small glimpse you gave me the other night, I can't imagine wanting you to be anyone else."

I smiled a sad smile as I tried to explain. "What

you saw the other night" —I shrugged in his grasp—
"I don't know if that was me or who that was. Being
with you in the privacy of our snow globe let me
be...someone I've never been. That's the thing, Van. I
don't know for sure who I am. That's why I came up
here to Ashland. I envisioned the person who listed
the job to be an old man with war stories he wanted
compiled."

Van smiled. "I'm not that old."

That made me smile too. "Considering that I
envisioned gray hair, wrinkles, and a frail stature, you,
Mr. Sherman, are about as far from what I imagined
as I could get."

"Are you disappointed?"

I shook my head. "Not in the least. The thing is, I
thought that by coming here I would get time to
evaluate my life and my decisions as I listened to the
old war stories and wrote."

I turned back to the window, captivated by the
sun's sparkles on the blanket of white snow.

Somehow this man, who I barely knew, understood more about my recent feelings and actions than
anyone. I spoke without looking at Van. "I know that
some people will think that my walking away from
my commitment to Skylar is impulsive—it wasn't.
Problems within my relationship with him had been
building since the moment I'd accepted his proposal
or even before."

Van stayed near, not speaking as my thoughts ran around my mind.

My discontent with Skylar grew similar to unattended brush fires, burning until they combined and created a massive blaze. Perhaps the grand-production proposal created the first spark. I didn't complain about Skylar's lack of sincerity, accepting the show for what it was.

More sparks added to the flames.

When Skylar and I tried to get close, the lack of attraction in his touch ate at me, making me wonder if our intimate life would change once I said I do and had the wedding ring upon my finger. I never mentioned it.

More flames ignited.

With each question that I asked myself, the fire of destruction threatened our forever. Beth's pregnancy didn't create the whole of the dissolution of Skylar and me. Her announcement was simply the final injection of fuel.

I met Van's stare. "Walking away from Skylar wasn't impulsive. Accepting your proposal was. It was wrong and impulsive."

"It was impulsive. Asking was impulsive," Van admitted, his deep voice filling me with warmth much like our time in the cabin. "It wasn't wrong. I've never proposed before. I've never had a grand plan of marrying to gain power."

"Is that what you'd gain by marrying me?"

"Yes. And so would you. However, just as you said, you don't need the money that comes with my job listing. I also don't need additional power. I have power. I have a lot of it. That doesn't stop me from wanting more."

"And again, what would you gain by marrying me?"

"There would be the obvious controlling majority stock share in Wade. That's only the tip of the iceberg. Since you and I spent the night together and I saw your name on the résumé, I've felt more alive than I have in years. That's you, Julia. I don't know how to define it, but whatever it is, I don't want to let it go. Concocting this plan to marry, acquiring the shares of Wade, the whole process has invigorated me in a way I haven't felt in longer than I can remember. It's made me see what could be, what I've missed in life by closing myself off. Now that I've seen it" —his smile grew— "now that I've had it in my hands, I don't want to let it go."

"What do you want?"

"You."

Me.

"Why do you want me?"

"Let's forget for a moment that you're brave and adventurous, taking on a snowstorm by yourself, or that you're intelligent and determined, or that you're beautiful" —his gaze shimmered— "dressed as you are now and even more so wearing my shirt or how spectacular you are when you're wearing nothing at all. For those reasons alone, I'd want you."

My breathing quickened as my pulse followed suit.

I wasn't sure how Van did it, how he made me feel all the things he was saying or how his tenor and words twisted my core with memories.

"Following through on this marriage," he went on, "will allow both of us to explore the more intimate part of our relationship, at the same time watch the Butlers fall, and save Wade Pharmaceutical."

I couldn't concentrate on my attraction to Van or my desire to explore an intimate world with him. If I did, I blurred the line between personal interest and business. I tried to deliberate on the details of Van's plan. "Is that who you are, Donovan Sherman, and what you do—you save companies?"

"No, it's not who I am. I do the opposite."

"Why do you care about Wade?"

"I don't."

"What do you care about," I asked, "or is there a who?"

"There's not a who. I told you, I've never proposed."

I shook my head. "I don't believe you. Everyone has a who."

"You can learn my past as you write my story."

I held tightly to the ribbon and crossed my arms over my breasts. "I've been a pawn in the McGrath-Butler connection for too long. And that makes me leery. This whole recent chain of events seems calculated."

Van stepped closer, cupped my chin, and lifted my eyes to his. The power I'd felt the first time we touched, sitting before the blazing fire, came back with a vengeance, sending small detonations throughout my circulation.

I was undeniably attracted to this man in a way that was new to me.

"The recent chain of events does seem unbelievable," Van agreed. "I'll give you that, but calculated, no. The last thing I planned on doing the other night was to find a beautiful, half-frozen woman in a snowstorm." He reached out to my cheek. "Or for the two of us to—"

I interrupted, "I don't regret the sex. You said I would. I don't. Regardless of my better-thought-out answer to your proposal, I'm not sorry for one minute about what we did. I told you then I had no expectations and laid no claims to you or to a future." As Van began to speak, I placed a finger on his full lips. "That night helped me more than you'll ever know. Being with you gave me a glimpse into what's beyond the constraints I've allowed to be placed on my life. That night with you, I broke free, and even in a snowstorm, I proved to myself that I was capable of surviving beyond the road map that had been drawn for me. Sex was another barrier that I broke that night."

Van reached for my hand, moving it away from his mouth as a smile came to his lips. "Technically, I think I was the one who broke..." He let the sentence end as his eyebrows moved up and down.

"I didn't come to Ashland looking for sex, to give away my virginity, or for another marriage proposal. I came here because of your job listing. All the coincidences..." I took a step back and away from his magnetic pull. "They seem..." I wasn't sure how to describe them.

"That listing has been open for three months," Van said. "You're the first candidate to show for an interview. The rest have all been frightened off by the unknown."

"Should I be frightened?"

Van nodded with a striking grin. "Very, but not in a bad way. You, Julia, should be exhilarated, excited, and filled with anticipation about the unknown. You said you were looking for a new life. Here it is. All you have to do is jump in with both feet. I'm not going to deny that the chain of events has occurred quickly. Call it fate, destiny, or cosmic irony. Whatever the greater power is that brought you to me and me to you was beyond either of our control. I believe my grandmother called it red sin."

My head tilted. "Red sin?"

"She said it was an old legend. Red is the color of blood, sacrifice, danger, and courage. It's also associated with heat, passion, and sexuality. When two people meet unexpectedly with an unexplainable attraction that defies common understanding, it's called red sin."

"Does that make it bad?" I asked, intrigued.

"My grandmother would say that bad is what you make out of what you're given. So is good. I never believed in red sin before you. Now, I can't deny that it's real. What we do with it is what will eventually define its goodness or badness. Am I alone, Julia? Do you not feel the same thing?"

"I do." I took a deep breath. "I'm attracted. I don't love you."

"Is that instrumental in marriage? Do you love Butler?"

I took another step back and spun in a slow circle. "That's not a fair question. Skylar and I have known one another our entire lives."

"Yet you were going to marry him, a man you've known your whole life, were never intimate with, and can't admit to loving."

"We were intimate. We just never—"

Van stepped closer, reaching for my waist and

holding my hips against his hard, muscular body. "Any man who has spent his life near you, Julia, and hasn't wanted or pursued the divine pleasure of being inside you isn't a man who's honest with you or with himself."

"We had an agreement."

"An agreement. We could have one of those too."

Chapter 08

Julia

*V*an's hold of me was distracting as he pulled me into his orbit. It would be too easy to stay within his gravitational pull, to give into the red sin. Thoughts of everything we've said cycloned within my mind. One thing in particular came to the top of my thoughts. I laid my hand on his chest, my fingers splaying over his satin tie. Beneath my touch, I felt the steady beat of his heart.

"Regardless of how attracted I am or how much I enjoyed the sex, I don't want to marry you simply because I'll regret the decision to marry you less than I would if I'd married Skylar. That's what you said. The lesser of two evils isn't the best choice."

With one arm snaked around my waist, Van tugged my hand with the ribbon and pried open my fingers. "Maybe it isn't red sin, but as you said, the white ribbon. One thing you should know about me is that I'm not the lesser of anyone or anything, including evils. I am that wolf you heard howling at the moon. Skylar Butler is an infant in the world of business. His father is a faltering piranha and Skylar is learning."

I stared at the ribbon lying in a twist on my palm and back up to his gaze. "How do you know so much about the Butlers?"

"I pay attention. The world of high finance has relatively few significant players."

"The Butlers are significant." I wasn't sure if I was stating or asking.

"No. They want to be."

"My family?"

"Are they significant? No, but they could be."

I tilted my head and looked up at Van. As his vibrant green stare searched mine, I shook my head and handed the ribbon back, placing it in his large palm. "I'm still sticking with my second answer. I can't jump with two feet into what I just escaped." Taking a step away, I freed myself from the warmth of Van's hold and I took a seat at the long table. "Tell me more about the job, about writing your memoir."

Van's gaze narrowed as he pulled out another chair and folded himself into the seat beside me at the head of the table. It was impossible not to notice how handsome Donovan Sherman was in his expensive suit covering the muscles and toned body that only a few nights ago had been against mine.

"Are you saying," he asked, "that you want the job, but not the proposal?"

"I'm not sure what I want," I answered honestly. "You read me right the other night in the cabin. You said that somewhere there's a man who did me wrong. You said that I was searching for a life that wasn't planned out, and in the process, I ended up stranded in a snowstorm.

"It was all true. Skylar Butler hurt me, but he's not the only one. I've allowed it. I've let others run my life for too long. I'm only twenty-four years old. My shares of Wade will remain under my father's oversight until I marry. I'm not in a hurry to do that, Van." I laid my hands out on the table, noticing my ring-free finger. "Besides, the idea that I have to marry to receive control of my shares is archaic and misogynistic. If I wanted, I could fight the will in court. Times have changed since my grandfather died."

"You could, but that will take time. Marlin Butler had immediate plans for Wade Pharmaceutical. I slowed those plans down with the purchase of the shares I bought this morning, but if you leave your shares under your father's control and Butler manages to connive your father into doing something unexpected, your family could lose everything. Butler currently has twenty-five percent." Van shook his head. "Did you wonder how I was able to acquire twenty-one percent as fast as I did?"

"Yes...no." I took a breath and released it. "I should have wondered. I haven't exactly been thinking straight."

"I was able to move fast because I have people working for me who constantly watch for instabilities in the market, in industries, and in businesses of all sizes. They watch for weaknesses that could lead to opportunities. Wade Pharmaceutical as well as other small pharmaceutical companies has been on our radar for some time. As I'm sure you're aware, recent pharmaceutical developments regarding patents, fast-tracked approval, and the government trying to regulate the prices of medications have all worked together to create a volatile environment. Your father is right about the bigger companies wanting to dominate the market. In most cases they do. Their size alone gives them the advantage. The twenty-one percent of Wade I just purchased was lined up for acquisition by Marlin Butler through multiple investment brokers." Van looked at his watch. "I would suspect that very soon, your ex-future father-in-law will realize I outbid him and stole the nest egg he planned to fry. His deals were interestingly timed."

My thoughts were now on Wade Pharmaceutical, the company my great-grandfather founded. In this short time, Van was telling me more than I'd ever gotten from my father or my grandfather before him.

"What do you mean, interestingly timed?" I asked.

"The sales were scheduled to go down at the end of business on December 30th. He'd placed a marker and paid a hefty fee to keep the deals hidden until then."

"December 30th? Skylar's and my wedding was supposed to be on the 31st, New Year's Eve."

Van nodded. "The 30th is also a Friday. The markets never truly close, but with the combination of the insignificance of Wade, the end of the fiscal year, and the holidays, there would have been a good chance that the news of the sales would have stayed hidden until return to business on January 3rd."

My mind was too busy trying to make sense of everything to concentrate on Van's description of Wade Pharmaceutical as insignificant.

I took a deep breath and stood. "Skylar and I would have been out of the country by then. Why should I believe you? If everything you say about Marlin Butler is true, then I've been a pawn longer than I realized. That doesn't instill trust. If I can't trust a man I've known my entire life, who is also my father's best friend, then how can I trust you? I don't even know you."

Van's gaze followed me as I walked back and forth

in front of the window. For a moment, I stared again out on the scenic snow-covered setting. As I watched people walk this way and that upon the sidewalks before the storefronts bundled in their winter layers, I realized there were many things I didn't know about Van, Ashland, or the company that was destined to be mine.

Before either of us could comment, a knock came at the door. When Van and I turned, Mr. Fields appeared.

"Oscar," Van said, "I said that we weren't to be disturbed."

Mr. Fields's gaze went from Van to me and back to Van. "Sir, if you'd like me to conclude this meeting for you, I'd be happy—"

"I don't."

"The time...it has taken—"

Van shook his head. "Call my office and let them know that I was detained."

"Do you have any idea of how long this meeting will last? Mrs. Preston called and you have another meeting..."

Taking a deep breath, Van stood. "Leave us. I'll call Connie."

Oscar Fields nodded as he backed out of the room and closed the door.

"What do you do?" I asked as Van reached for the phone in his breast pocket.

His full lips curled as his gaze met mine. "I buy and sell."

"What?"

"Anything. Everything has a price." Van lifted his phone to his ear. Still speaking to me, he said, "Move in with me, write my memoir, and learn who I really am."

It was an intriguing offer.

What will I learn?

Who is this man who is a self-proclaimed significant player in the world of high finance, who dresses as if he is to appear on Esquire, and also chops wood and is comfortable in a remote cabin?

He called Skylar an infant. From what I'd seen of Van, I couldn't judge his age. His statement would mean that he was older than Skylar and older than I.

How much?

Van's attention went to the person on the other end of the phone call. "Connie, I've had a change of plans. Cancel the rest of my day." He paused. "I agree." His green gaze scanned from my head to my toes as a smile curled his lips. "This is highly unusual." He disconnected the call.

"Who are you?" I asked.

His gaze glistened like fine emeralds. "Accept my offer and find out. Do you accept?"

"The job offer or the marriage proposal?"

"Accept the job offer," Van said, "and we'll put the

proposal of marriage on hold. Those are my terms. If you want the job, the proposal won't be taken back nor will I accept your second answer. Your first instinct, Julia, was to say yes. You want time to discover yourself. Take that time to let me do the same. And you can get to know me."

"What about sex?" I asked.

"The job comes with your own living quarters."

"Does that mean no sex?"

"I'd like to leave that subject open for debate. If you agree, we can get to know one another as we explore the more personal aspects of a relationship."

I took a deep breath.

Is this exactly why I left Chicago?

Is red sin the new life I haven't known I am searching for?

"Julia?"

"A new life."

Van nodded.

"I think I owe it to myself to see what it entails."

"Does that mean...?"

"It means that yes, Van, I accept."

Chapter
09

Julia

Somehow during my drive along the white ribbon, I'd gotten off the main road. At least my GPS had kept me on roads. The road I followed took me west of Ashland. That was how I ended up on the outskirts of Van's property. If I would have continued, instead of crashing into a snowbank, I would have reached Lake Superior. Now after accepting Van's offer of exploring the job opportunity, I was following his large black truck northwest from Ashland to the west side of Chequamegon Bay.

The country and land near the shores of the Great Lake were stunning, even with their white covering. Tall trees of all varieties reached up to the blue sky. Though the snow had stopped, the massive accumulation of lake-effect snow now appeared as tall white walls on the sides of plowed roads, ones that were barely wide enough for two-way traffic.

Following in Van's truck's tracks, I scolded myself

for not accepting his offer of a ride to his house. If it weren't for the tracks from his truck, barreling through the snow that had blown back onto the roads, I was skeptical as to whether the car I rented would be able to proceed.

Once we'd passed through Washburn, a quaint little city even smaller than Ashland, we were back onto narrow roads in wilderness. If I chose to stay in this area, for the job or any other offer, it would take me some time to get used to the difference between here and the city of Chicago.

Gone were the big buildings and traffic jams.

The road I was following wound through the tall trees until we arrived at a lane with an open gate, leading to what I assumed was Donovan Sherman's home. Following his truck, I drove up a winding, inclined lane. My mouth opened as I stared through the windshield, taking in the huge structure. By its sheer size alone, I wondered if at one point this had been a hotel or bed and breakfast. At the same time, it appeared modern with a lot of windows and a combination stone and wood-sided exterior.

With the rental car parked on the cleared wide driveway, I stepped from the car and lifted my face to the massive structure. Pulling my down jacket around me, I stuffed my hands into the pockets to shield myself from the cold. I turned slowly all the way around, taking in the way the structure surrounded three sides of the driveway.

The closing of Van's truck door echoed from the garages on my left. I turned, noticing how different he appeared from the night I met him. His mountain-man clothing was replaced with his custom-fitted suit and covered by a double-breasted wool coat. Instead of boots he wore leather loafers that clipped upon the concrete as he walked toward me from one of the double garages, the one where he'd just parked his truck. His orange hat was nowhere to be seen, and his gelled dark mane blew in the breeze.

I took in the other two double garage doors. Both sides of the structure were two stories, the center was three. Turning, it appeared as if the middle structure was the main house with another wing to the right and one to the left.

"This is a lot of house for one man."

"I suppose it is."

Van placed his hand in the small of my back. "Come with me and let me show you around."

"Said the spider to the fly," I mumbled as the pressure of his too-familiar touch brought thoughts of another part of our agreement to mind.

Without replying, Van led me up the front stone porch to the large entry. The door before us was easily five feet taller than Van. It was odd to see him appear dwarfed. That hadn't happened in the cabin or Mr. Fields's office. He turned the large knob and pushed the door inward.

We entered a foyer with a high ceiling and a uniquely beautiful lighting fixture above. To one side was an elegant built-in hall tree. It wasn't the kind that was freestanding, but rather integrated ornate woodwork, easily six feet wide with a bench, storage areas, and hooks. There was a louvered door to the right. Van opened it, offering to take my coat and hang it in the front closet. As he hung my outer coat and his, I peered at what was awaiting me beyond this enclosed entry, my curiosity piqued.

The house was blockaded by an exquisite set of tall French doors, the interior distorted by the leaded-glass panels. Van's hand was again on my lower back as he opened the French doors.

I wasn't unaccustomed to the finer things in life. The home where I was raised in Lincoln Park had been in our family for two generations. My mother's parents, the son of her grandfather who founded Wade Pharmaceutical, purchased the home for nearly half a million. Fifty years later it was easily worth ten million. The six-bedroom limestone structure was every bit as grand as it had been when it first came to our family.

However, as Van opened the front door and we

stepped inside, I was impressed with the understated elegance I saw before me. The floor plan, as well as the furnishings, was the perfect combination of opulent and rustic. The tiled entry within gave way to glistening wood floors, open rounded archways to both sides, and a large room beyond with pillars. The staircase curved upward to the second-story landing and beyond to a third story. Both levels and the staircase had railings and a banister with a shiny wood handrail and wrought-iron railing spindles.

"As you can see," he said, "there's plenty of space."

Making my way beyond the entry, I saw the main level was open and spacious. I was drawn into the large living room and over to the wall of windows peering out over the bay. The water was frosted by snow, covering the ice under the tranquil sky. "This view is lovely."

"It's a bit different from Chicago's skyline."

I nodded, still mesmerized by the pristine snow covering.

"I appreciate the isolation," Van said.

Turning one way and the next, I searched for other homes. "How much land do you have?"

"Not as much as I'd like."

A smile tugged at my lips. "Earlier you said you want more power. Now you want more land. Will you ever have enough?"

He inhaled as he shrugged. "I suppose some see it

as greed, but that's not how I see it." His eyes moved from me to the beautiful scene beyond the windows. "I'm also not unsatisfied. I believe that the quest for more and better is because there is always something more, something newer, a fresh challenge. I think that living a life without the need for the next step would be uninspired. What would be the point of waking without a goal for each day?"

"Some people set satisfaction as their end goal. Once they achieve it, they enjoy it."

Van shook his head as he turned to me. "It's the pursuit I enjoy."

"So if I had agreed to marry you, I'd no longer be enjoyable? You'd want to move on to another?"

"No, Julia, that isn't what I said. You see, having you agree to marry me would be the first step in our relationship. I would pursue you to have more, better, the unknown, and even the unobtainable." He started to reach for my cheeks; before he did, Van pulled his hands back and straightened his lips. "Let me show you around more."

I reached for his hand; the warmth radiated from him to me. "What were you going to say?"

He squeezed my hand and let our connection sever. "It's irrelevant."

"Tell me anyway."

The ends of Van's lips curled. "One day, Miss McGrath. Currently, you agreed to an employer-employee relationship. It would be highly inappropriate for me to tell you what I was thinking while under those titles."

My grin blossomed on my face. "Perhaps you should share your human resource officer's name with me. I may need to make a complaint."

"If you take this position, you won't be employed by Sherman and Madison Corporation or any of its subsidiaries. I'm afraid the agreement will be strictly between you and me."

"If I have a complaint?"

"Bring it to me," he said.

"And if you are unsatisfied with my work?"

The golden flecks in his green eyes became more apparent. "If it's your inexperience you're concerned about, I don't find that a problem. While it was surprising, I've given it some thought, and I find myself attracted to it."

Why did I tell him I was a virgin?

It was because I thought I'd never see him again.

I feigned the professionalism I'd thought we were discussing. However, as warmth crept from my chest, up my neck, and to my cheeks, I doubted I was pulling off the facade. "I wasn't talking about that."

Van's eyes opened wider. "Your résumé states you're unpublished and the only writing you've completed was for your minor at Northwestern. Do you have more experience in writing memoirs than you mentioned?"

My eyes blinked. "No, yes, you're right." *Why do I think he is talking about sex?* Maybe it was my mind that kept going there. "I don't have a lot of experience in writing memoirs. I understand if that makes me unqualified."

"I've read my share of memoirs. Some are formulistic and dry. Your lack of experience interests me because I've found that the less experienced individual relies more upon their passion. It's that inner drive that pushes them forward. Mistakes may or may not be made, but those are usually in the mechanics, easily fixable. Over time that passion tends to lessen. The finished products become more cookie cutter. Insert information here and there. That isn't what I want for this project. I'm attracted to your passion, Julia."

I sucked in a breath, still unsure about the blurred line between the memoir and sex.

Van went on, "You accepted my offer. And for the record, I don't anticipate being unhappy with your performance—"

"Writing performance," I clarified.

He smirked. "Yes, that is what we're discussing, right?"

"Right."

"If I'm unsatisfied in any way or you are, together

we'll work it out, simple mechanics. As a point of interest, your manuscript will not only need to be approved by me, but it will also need to go through a vetting process with my legal team."

"Why?"

"It's nothing about your writing. It's the content. I've been involved in many ventures that if mentioned in our conversations should not be part of the final manuscript. If those matters are mentioned, the legal team will redact them from your work."

I wasn't certain how to respond.

Instead, I turned back to the large living room we'd traversed on our way to the windows.

While the furnishings were stunning, it was the grand piano that first caught my eye. Walking toward it, I gently ran my fingers over the ivory keys, not applying enough pressure to sound even one note. When I looked up, Van was looking at me with an unreadable expression.

"Do you play?" I asked.

"I used to. Do you?"

A bashful smile came to my lips. "It's been a while. I was never that good."

"I'm not used to having others around, but if playing this piano will help you think and thinking will change your answer to my proposal, then by all means, you're welcome to play. I have it tuned yearly." He leaned down as his large fingers splayed over the keys, rounding to the perfect position and began to play.

The room filled with a sad melody. Music rang out as within the piano, small hammers struck their corresponding strings, sending the tune reverberating through the open room. I was enthralled by the way Van's hands moved, effortlessly flying over the keys. The tune only lasted a few seconds. He'd only played a few bars and still, I recognized the complicated piece.

"Beethoven," I said, my mouth still opened with awe.

"You have a good ear. 'Moonlight Sonata.'"

"That was amazing. Why did you say you no longer play?"

"The answer to that question very well could be an example of what is not to be exposed in my memoir." Van reached for the cover and pulled it down over the keys. "You're welcome to play this piano whenever you want."

"My ability is nothing compared to yours. Maybe listening to you play will help me think."

"I'll give you the Wi-Fi information. Feel free to stream any music you desire."

Mentally I was making a list of the things I wanted to learn about Donovan Sherman. That list was growing by the second.

"Let me show you to your suite."

As we began walking toward the front staircase, Van said, "I wasn't planning on the job applicant living in my home. I never intended to have contact with the writer. I have notes and files. It was my plan to share the information and then allow the writer to pen the compilation."

"What? The ad said to live on-site."

"When deciding to begin this endeavor, I'd anticipated *on-site* to mean on my property. You asked how much land I have. It's a little over seventy acres." He took a deep breath. "You, Julia McGrath, have other attributes besides the writing of the memoir. In a rather selfish decision, I changed my plans, deciding I wanted you closer. However, in all fairness, if you have any misgivings about living here with me, there's a guesthouse on my property not far away, and then also..." —he grinned— "well, you remember the cabin."

My cheeks rose. "Yes, I remember the cabin. I also remember that it doesn't have electricity. That would make charging my laptop difficult."

"I'll show you your suite. When I had this house refurbished, I did so with the idea that each suite was self-contained with a sitting room, bedroom, and en suite bathroom." He pointed to the ceiling at least fifteen feet above. "Mine is upstairs closest to the garages. I'll show you to the one at the farthest end of the south wing. Next to mine, it has the best view of the bay."

Shall I look for a message in Van's desire to have me farther away?

Then again, is the suite far when the other option is a guesthouse?

10

Van

*C*ontinuing up the staircase, I gripped the banister as we came to the second-story landing and I peered down to the first floor. Visions from the past floated past my mind's eye. They were recollections I'd successfully kept buried for years, memories I forbade myself from reliving while keeping them close enough to serve as a warning for my future.

It was impulsive of me to propose to Julia. The phone in my breast pocket was receiving one voice-mail message after another from my legal counsel as well as others who knew me, all in the name of stopping me from making a mistake.

Another mistake.

Waking beside Julia in the cabin was surreal.

How long has it been since I've spent the night—the entire night—with a woman?

A decade.

More than that.

Over a decade, not that I consciously kept count. That didn't mean I was celibate. It meant that I didn't open myself up for what came after sex.

I peered down at the first floor again. The structure around me had changed, but the memory was right there, close enough that if I ran down the flight of stairs, I could stop...

"Van?" Julia asked, her voice scattering my thoughts. "Are you all right?"

I shook my head, dispersing the accumulated clutter that builds with time, knocking down the cobwebs veiling the memories, and dislodging the dust that dulled the colors until red was no longer deep and flowing.

I feigned a smile. "It's been a long time since I've escorted anyone new around my house."

Julia's blue eyes glowed as she peered over the banister and up to the third level. "What's up there?"

"Nothing really."

"You have an entire floor for nothing?"

It wasn't nothing. At one time it had been everything. "With over ten thousand square feet, there's a lot of room for nothing."

"How many bedroom suites?" she asked.

"Five, all on this level," I added.

Julia's head shook. "Why so much space?"

"Because it's never enough."

Her smile dimmed. It wasn't a radical change in

her beautiful expression, but I saw the way the light in her eyes faded. "Is that the title of your memoir —*never enough?*"

"I think that one is taken."

"Every title is taken. When we add the byline 'Memoir of Donovan Sherman,' it will be unique." She looked down the multiple hallways. From the landing there were three options that didn't include up or down. To the far left was the hallway leading to my suite. In the center, two more suites could be reached. And to the far right, another two, including the one I had in mind for Julia.

"When I purchased the house, I had it gutted, expanded, and redone," I said. "Suites seemed to be the thing to build. My architect believed that should I decide to sell, the suites would increase its value, making it a viable bed and breakfast. I'm not interested in selling." I reached for her hand. As we touched one another, I immediately regretted my move and let our connection drop.

Even so, the tingle remained.

Red sin.

"This way," I said, leading the way to the south wing, my thoughts filled with the woman at my side.

From the first time I saw Julia standing half-frozen along the road, I was pulled toward her. In all honesty, it happened before I saw her. It was as I found her car.

Never in my life had I been called a hero nor did I deserve that title. Never did I seek out the stranded or misguided to lead them to the straight and narrow path of goodness and safety. My motives were usually more self-gratifying and less altruistic.

And yet seeing the empty car buried in the snow-bank, I felt an unexplainable urgency to search. With worsening conditions, when a sane man would have driven to the safety of his home, I slowed my speed and peeled my eyes through the darkening sky and blinding blizzard.

I didn't know her name nor did she know mine, and yet once she was in my arms and I laid her down in my truck, I wanted to keep her.

A saying from my childhood came to mind: finders keepers.

I found her.

Julia was mine, and I wasn't going to let her go.

Over the last eleven years, I'd reined in that all-consuming desire.

I'd refocused my needs away from the unthinkable to the goal of obtaining *things*. It didn't matter what—I wanted it and took it.

I'd concentrated day and night on what I did well and made what I did better, more profitable, superior and grander than before. As I pushed to succeed, the name Sherman, one that was barely known or recognized, became equated with power and savvy in the world of high finance. Fifty-million-dollar deals became one hundred million. One hundred million became one billion. I moved up and over those blocking my path toward success.

I made enemies.

Some enemies became friends.

Others remain embroiled in their adversarial role.

Or perhaps it was me who was the adversary.

It's the way I preferred to see it.

On the offensive, the predator ready to attack.

In general, I kept my distance, always appearing as the facade of the man society required me to be. The cloak of normality grew heavy at times, too heavy to maintain.

This home became my retreat, my place away from the world, a place where I could safely examine and overcome those things that needed to stay hidden.

It wasn't because bringing light to that darkness would endanger my career—although it would. It was because to succeed in this world, one must be the lion appearing as the gazelle—quick and sure-footed, aware of one's surroundings, and gentle enough to approach.

Is that the way Julia sees me—safe to approach?

I wasn't.

Am I simply luring her closer for the kill?

I didn't know. This was unfamiliar territory.

My senses were on alert.

Everything about her stimulated them—the perfection of her beauty, the scent of her perfume, the energy in her touch, the melody of her voice, and the memory of her taste.

Will having her present alter my mission for better and more, or will I find that drive also applies to Julia?

My need to succeed was my reason to wake each morning. I required that incentive to move beyond the darkness. This house provided my solitude and a place where I could allow myself to slip into the shadows.

That was why Julia should also rescind her decision to accept my offer.

She should move to the guesthouse or back to Chicago.

My home was a bubble where I kept the memories that mattered without any outward sign of those people, places, or things having ever existed. It was also secluded. I'd orchestrated that on purpose by buying five- and ten-acre lots and demolishing most structures.

It was easier to keep urges suppressed when there wasn't another soul for miles.

I wasn't a hermit.

I interacted with people at the office, in meetings here in northern Wisconsin, around the country, and around the world. I traveled and played nice, always with the plan to make it back here to face my demons alone.

Few people entered my bubble though I did have help.

Mrs. Mayhand, a widowed woman I'd known for a long time, came to the house once a week while I wasn't home and filled my refrigerator and freezer with a week's worth of easy-to-warm meals. Her daughter, Margaret Curry, drove Mrs. Mayhand, and while her mother cooked, Margaret cleaned the unlocked rooms. Jonathon, Margaret's husband, cared for the landscaping near the house. This time of year that meant he plowed my lane and driveway. During the spring, summer, and autumn, he tended to the lawns and other landscaping. Farther away, beyond the main house and the nearby structures, the surrounding acres were left to nature.

If a tree fell, it remained a habitat to house chip-munks, mice, snakes, and insects. Pine needles and leaves fell in the autumn and created nutrition for the undergrowth. Saplings sprang to life wherever their roots held them. Wolves, foxes, and deer were some of the more prominent mammals that called my land home.

I preferred them to the two-legged kind.

There were few people I trusted enough to allow them inside my bubble.

As I peered down at Julia by my side and as we

passed the locked door of another suite, I couldn't come up with a reason why I'd chosen to trust her and invite her into a place where so few had been welcome. I didn't know Julia McGrath and yet as we briefly touched only moments ago, it was as it had been upon seeing her car, as if a gravitational pull existed between the two of us, two masses in motion lured toward one another.

My negative energy was attracted to Julia's positive energy and—I believed—vice versa. In physics, our speed would increase, drawing us closer, faster and faster until neither of us could slow the progression. Ultimately, we'd collide, the cosmic blast decimating everything within its pull.

Julia and I came to a stop at the final door as I turned the doorknob and pushed inward.

A smile came to my face as I peered around. When this plan to keep Julia began to take shape in my thoughts, one of the calls I made was to Margaret, asking her to make a special trip to my home to freshen this room. She seemed so surprised that I might have a guest that she assured me she would get it done. I didn't think about the fact that I was asking her to travel up my twisty lane following a snowstorm.

Margaret didn't complain.

Now, seeing the glistening wood of the tables in

the sitting room and the open curtains throughout the suite, I knew she'd done as she promised.

"It's beautiful," Julia said.

I walked to the window in the sitting room beyond the fireplace. Pushing the drapery to the side, I stared out at the frozen bay. "You can see the bay from here and from the balcony in the bedroom."

Julia ran her hand over the leather loveseat near the fireplace. "This looks new."

"Not new, just not used."

I followed a few steps behind as she went from room to room, stopping at the doorway to the bathroom as she examined the updated amenities, the marble tile and glistening chrome. I also stopped at the entry of the bedroom, watching as she roamed around, peering into the closet and out onto the balcony. "Have you changed your mind?" I asked, wanting her to say yes and saying a silent prayer to an unknown entity that she'd say no.

Julia took a deep breath.

As she did, the way her pert breasts pushed against her white blouse and the muscles in her neck strained, creating that sexy V near her collarbone, caught my attention. I scanned lower, to where her black slacks accentuated her trim waist.

My thoughts went back to the night when I'd undressed her unconscious body.

Today she was a strong and capable woman.

That night, she'd been a fragile bird in need of care.

That night, it took all my willpower to not peer beneath the bra and panties.

In doing so, I'd shown Julia the restraint I'd lacked with others. This beautiful angel deserved better than a man like me. She'd said that she was twenty-four. That made me nearly two decades her senior, and yet, as that night progressed, the unthinkable occurred. Julia came back to life, a vibrant beacon calling to me and inviting me into her orbit. Now that I was here, I didn't want to break free.

Contemplating my question, Julia paced, stepping upon the floors and rugs in her high heels as if she were bred to move in a graceful manner. Given what I now know of her family, she had been.

Julia McGrath had been placed on this earth to secure her, her family's, and Wade's future.

Instead of doing that, she was here in my home with a man capable of destroying her and her family's business.

I heard the warning bells.

Much like sirens from the lighthouses out upon the Apostle Islands, the ones in my mind were cautioning of the danger that lay ahead.

The words were on the tip of my tongue. I would tell her that my offer of a job was rescinded. I would help her find her way back to Ashland and back to Chicago.

Before I could voice my thoughts, Julia spoke, "I don't want the guesthouse, Van." Her smile lit up the bedroom. "I want time to think, but being alone in your guesthouse would be too lonely. This suite is beautiful. And," she added, "I'll have company."

"Maybe you should reconsider the entire offer."

"I have. I don't know what brought me here, whether it was cosmic irony or what your grandmother called red sin, but I can't deny that I too am interested in both you and this opportunity, too interested to walk away. I'll contact my parents. After the first of the year, I'll go back to Chicago and find out what's happening with Wade Pharmaceutical. I think that after what I found out about Skylar, I want to stay far away from Chicago beyond the wedding date and let the dust settle."

Maybe Julia was right with what she said earlier.

She was the fly and I was the spider.

Or maybe I was right—Julia was the innocent doe, wide-eyed on unsteady knees and I was the wolf. Either way, she'd just been invited to my web or my den.

Given her acceptance, with time she would come to regret her decision.

Forty-one years had taught me one thing I couldn't deny. I knew myself. I knew what I was capable of doing. I also knew that I hadn't felt this way around a woman in a long time. Perhaps I was wrong about my doomsday outlook. Maybe time had tamed the beast within me. Over ten years had passed since I let the beast win.

I had to believe that Julia was different and I could control the man I'd been.

This agreement would end up either very good or very bad.

Time held the answer.

"I haven't changed my mind. I'll take the job," she said with a smile.

My cold heart didn't know if it should leap with joy or sink with despair. It wasn't easy to have hope when for so long it had been an elusive bitch. And yet staring down at Julia's blue kaleidoscope within her expressive orbs, I told myself that this relationship would end differently.

After all, it had begun differently.

Life wasn't a loop such as the movie *Groundhog Day* would suggest.

This was a new chance.

"Then it's settled," I said. "Welcome."

Chapter 11

Julia

I stepped into the lobby of the hotel in Ashland. The large hotel was constructed on the shore of the Chequamegon Bay in 1877, by the Wisconsin Central Railroad interests. The stately wooden pillars and trim created an atmosphere that gave one the feeling of stepping back in time. Its central location within Ashland was perfect for visitors. It had been perfect for me, allowing me to peer out my window at the frozen bay and walk a few blocks to shops and restaurants.

With my mind on my decision to move in with Van, I wasn't paying attention. I should have been looking around at my surroundings. I wasn't.

"Julia."

I sucked in a breath at the familiar voice.

The counter ahead of me was empty. I turned toward the lobby, seeing the fireplace and furniture, and yet not one chair or sofa was occupied. I turned again in time to come face-to-face with Skylar Butler.

I'd never denied he was handsome; neither had he.

His dark blond hair was combed back. His khaki pants and brown loafers showed below the hem of his unbuttoned wool coat. The coat parted enough to see his patterned button-up shirt, undone at his neck. This was Skylar's idea of casual.

His blue eyes met mine. "Julia, we need to talk."

With my hands in the pockets of my coat, I stood taller. "Skylar, you didn't need to make this trip." My gaze narrowed. "How did you know where I was?"

He took a step closer. "I know you rented a car. We can return it here in Ashland and drive back to Chicago together. That will give us time to talk."

"I don't need time. I don't need to talk."

He looked around the lobby. "This doesn't need to be discussed in public." He motioned toward the elevators. "We could go to your room."

"Again, how did you know that I am staying here?"

"I don't love Beth."

I took a step backward.

I was currently within a scene from a bad movie. He was right, if we were to have this conversation, it shouldn't be in public, but then again, I didn't want the conversation to occur at all, and based on the emptiness of the large entry, there wasn't anyone to overhear.

I pointed toward the archway to the hotel's bar.

"We can go in the bar. I'll give you five minutes. No more."

His hand came to the small of my back as we turned to enter the bar.

I stepped away from his touch.

Despite the tacky neon sign advertising a popular brand of beer on the deep red walls, the room was as lovely as the entry. The long bar was heavy wood with ornate carvings on the front and lined with a brass handrail. Behind the bar was more elaborate wood-work centered around a lighted large mirror with shelves and hundreds of bottles of liquors and wines.

"I could buy you a drink," Skylar offered. His tone had an unusual sound of trepidation. It seemed as though his usual cockiness had given way to this new subdued and unsure attitude.

"I don't want a drink," I said, removing my coat and taking a seat at one of the tables.

Skylar also removed his coat, folded it meticulously, and draped it over one of the chairs before taking a seat beside me.

For a long moment, we simply stared at one another.

There had been too much time spent with one another not to have those memories swirling through my thoughts. And yet they didn't make my heart flutter or my mouth go dry as they did when I looked into Van's green orbs.

Skylar reached for my hand.

I looked at our connection, feeling the coolness of his skin, and for the first time recognizing the absence of more.

That too was because of Van.

He'd explained his ongoing desire for more and better.

Feeling the coolness of Skylar's touch, I came to the same decision. I deserved more. Now that I'd had a taste of more, I wouldn't settle for less.

My gaze met his. "I'm not changing my mind."

Skylar inhaled. "It's been four days. I thought if I let you burn off some steam, you'd come back. The wedding is only in a week and a half."

"There won't be a wedding, not with us." I feigned a smile as I looked at our hands and removed mine from his. "You said you don't love Beth. Do you love me?"

"Of course I do."

My nose scrunched. "Do you?"

"Why would you even question that? I've loved you my whole life."

"Have you ever been *in love* with me?"

He lowered his voice as the bartender came to the bar, peering our way. "Yes, Julia. I only want to spend forever with you."

"How many women have you slept with?"

He sat taller. "Why would you ask?"

"Because we never had sex. Don't you think that's odd?"

"We were waiting. If you don't think that I've thought about the gift you've saved for me, you're wrong."

I swallowed. "Skylar, I don't wish you unhappiness. I just don't wish for my unhappiness by spending my eternity with you."

His head moved from side to side. "Where is this coming from?"

A scoff escaped my throat. "You have a child coming."

"I don't believe her. Hell, that kid could belong to any one of five guys."

"And you're one of them." It was my gut reaction. My second was to defend my friend. Beth wasn't the slut Skylar was making her out to be. Nevertheless, I kept any defense suppressed. It wasn't my role to fight for Beth's relationship with my ex-fiancé.

"Julia, you're being ridiculous. You've known for years that I had a sex life. Once we're married, it will be only you."

"When you and Beth touch, do you feel a sensation like lightning through your body? When you see her, does your heart race? When you kiss does the world around you disappear?"

He shook his head. "No, you're talking like some stupid movie on Lifetime. That shit isn't real."

It was real.

I never knew it before, but now I did.

"Have you ever heard of red sin?"

The bartender appeared at our table. "What can I get you two?"

Before I could answer, Skylar spoke, "A glass of white moscato for the lady and two fingers of Angel's Envy, neat, for me."

"I don't—"

Skylar nodded and the man walked away.

Has Skylar always dismissed my choices and I never noticed?

Instead of belaboring that thought, I asked again, "Red sin?"

"No. I've never heard of it." He lowered his voice. "Let me help you get your things. We'll return the rental and if we get on the road, we can be back to Chicago by one."

"And you'll return me to my parents like the good fiancé?" I recalled Van's assessment of any man who would know me for my entire life and not want more.

"Yes, and after our wedding, we'll fly across the ocean and spend two weeks doing what I've dreamt about."

I smirked. "You've dreamt about making love to me? Was this before or after you fucked Beth and all the others?"

"Julia, I screwed up. I admit it. I don't love Beth.

I'm not sure if the kid she's carrying is even mine. If it is, I'll do the right thing and pay for her abortion."

My eyes opened wide. "The right thing?"

"I'm not sorry. The only children I want are ours."

Our drinks arrived.

I closed my fingers around the stem of the glass, contemplating my next move. As I swirled the light-colored liquid, tossing the contents in Skylar's face was moving higher on my list of possibilities.

"Julia, I want you to know that I'm committed to making our marriage work."

Taking a deep breath, I leveraged the table's edge as I pushed my chair back. "I'm not."

"You have cold feet. Ana said it's normal. She said you'll come around."

Ana was my mother. Her real name was Anastasia. She liked the longer version for business and social purposes. Being as Skylar had known her since he was born, to him, she was Ana.

"My feet are fine. I hope you'll reconsider the *right thing* when it comes to Beth. You're also correct; you screwed up. Now it's time to man up. I'm staying in Ashland. I've accepted a job."

Skylar stood.

I lifted my chin, keeping our eye contact.

Through the years, I'd seen most of my ex-fiancé's moods. If I were to predict, his steady, reassuring, and slightly self-deprecating position was about to give way to a more forceful demand. Skylar was a lot of things, but violent wasn't one of them. My reasoning for not inviting him to my hotel room wasn't because I feared him or because I was concerned he'd make inappropriate moves; he'd had reason for the first over time and never gone that way. As for the second, he'd had ample opportunity and failed.

My reasoning was simple.

I was done with this relationship.

"You can't be serious," he said. "You already have a job at Wade."

"I need time to let the dust settle. You do too. Take it. Our engagement is off. The wedding is canceled. I want you to leave."

He pulled a twenty and a ten from his money clip and laid them on the table. Lifting the glass with his whiskey, he downed the two fingers. "This could devastate Wade. Do you even care about your family business?"

Skylar was prepared to give me every guilt trip possible. The problem was that I wasn't guilty. He was. "Do I want my life to be a contract to keep control of my family's dream?" As I spoke the question, I realized the answer applied to more than Skylar and me but also to Van's proposal. "No. I do care. I just won't live my life regretting that decision."

I lifted my coat and began to walk away but turned back. "Drive safely, Skylar. As far as I'm concerned, your employment at Wade is secure. I suppose that isn't up to me right now, but I don't wish you ill. I simply have never been in love with you and am relieved I learned that sooner rather than later."

He came closer, reaching for my arm and pulling me toward him. His arm surrounded my waist as his lips took mine.

It took less than a second for the ice-cold connection to fuel my protest.

Using both hands, I pushed against Skylar's chest until he stepped back, tripping over one of the chairs. From the corner of my eye, I saw the bartender watching. No longer did I care what was overheard. "If you ever touch me like that again, I will personally see to it that you and your family are out of Wade. For the final time, we're done. Goodbye, Skylar."

With that, I turned, keeping my head high as I went to the elevator and hit the *up* button. When the doors opened, I stepped inside. As the doors closed, I made no effort to look beyond my own space. I didn't know if Skylar Butler had left the bar, was in the lobby, or had exited the hotel.

I didn't care.

As I gathered my things in the room, I decided to call down to the bar.

"Hello, this is Julia McGrath in room 426. Can

you tell me if the man with whom I was sharing a drink has left?"

"He's gone. I asked him to leave."

I let out a long sigh. "Thank you."

"Lady, are you in for the night?"

"I'm checking out."

"Before you head out to your car, stick your head in here and I'll send one of the busboys out with you."

"Thank you. I appreciate your assistance."

Chapter 12

Julia

I took comfort in the darkening sky and even in the new covering of snow that melted against my windshield and accumulated on the twisty lane as I drove back toward Van's home. After the run-in with Skylar, it truly felt liberating. This was a new world, and I had no doubt that I'd made the right decision.

The rental car was once again filled with my luggage, everything I'd brought with me from Chicago. I didn't have many changes of clothes, but that didn't even tempt me to return either alone or with Skylar to Chicago. Seeing Skylar was awkward enough; the thought of facing my parents or his caused my stomach to twist and turn.

I knew that I shouldn't feel that way. I wasn't the one who cheated on Skylar.

Will my parents see it that way if they know about Van?

I'd given that some thought as I'd packed. The

conclusion I'd come to was that I'd broken off the engagement before setting out on my quest.

I believed that meeting Van helped me to see that there was a bigger, brighter world beyond Chicago, the Butlers, and even Wade Pharmaceutical. Without that knowledge, it would have been more difficult to send Skylar back to Beth or whoever he had in store for his future. My thoughts were on my own future.

Perhaps I was reluctant to face those people back in Chicago because I wasn't remorseful about the canceled wedding. I felt bad for the money my parents had spent, but that was it. The brief conversation I'd had with my mother this afternoon before seeing Skylar reaffirmed my decision to stay away through the holidays.

Now I wondered if she knew Skylar was driving up here. After all, she'd pleaded with me to work things out with him. I held fast to my conviction when I spoke with her and with Skylar. Our wedding was canceled.

I didn't mention to her that I'd received a new marriage proposal or any other details about the recent events that led me to accept a job offer. To say that Mom was as shocked as Skylar when I told her that I took a job in Ashland would be an understatement.

When she asked for more detail, I was vague.

If Donovan Sherman was as big of a name as he

claimed—and he was because I did a quick internet search—then my father would recognize his name. I wasn't ready to have that conversation. Therefore, I purposely left Van's name out of our discussion.

For some reason, when Van and I met and were in the cabin, I hadn't thought too much about his age. I simply saw him for the incredibly handsome man who saved me, showed me that there's life beyond Chicago, and listened to my woes. Of course, with the intimate turn our night together took, I knew that he took care of himself. He also had stamina and experience and expertise in what women wanted.

While waiting to be sure Skylar was gone and doing a quick internet search of Donovan Sherman, I'd found a bio that listed Van as one of *Forbes* wealthiest men in the United States and at the same time gave very little personal information. I also learned the date he was born, letting me know that he was forty-one years old.

His financial status didn't surprise me.

His age did.

I couldn't decide if it bothered me.

If my age doesn't bother him, why should his bother me?

As I crested the hill, the golden lights from Van's home shone through the darkness, reminding me of a Thomas Kinkade painting. As the large structure came into view, a sense of peace settled over me combined with hopeful anticipation for what this reprieve from my real world would entail. The feelings were foreign, and I welcomed the thrill of the unexpected coursing through my circulation.

Red sin.

With my life's road map torn to shreds and left wadded in a trash can—especially after the encounter with Skylar—Van was an adventure upon which I was excited to embark.

Even though Van had proposed marriage, I wasn't certain that either of us wanted to go that far. I wasn't looking for forever. I'd had that promised to me and that promise meant nothing. What I sought from Van was the way I felt when I was with him. I was already addicted to the adrenaline rush, giddiness, and fluttering heart that came with each encounter.

As I pulled the car onto the large driveway, the front door opened. Van was no longer in his custom suit from earlier but wearing clothes such as he'd worn the first time I met him. There was nothing about him that made me think of him as old.

Putting the car in park, I subconsciously scanned from his dark hair down his wide shoulders and trim waist. The flannel shirt he wore over the thermal twisted my core in a way that brought warmth to my cheeks. I wouldn't need more clothes if Van had an ample supply of flannel shirts he'd be willing to share.

Then again, I'd agreed to the employee and

employer titles. I didn't suppose that included borrowing my employer's shirts to wear as a nightgown.

His smile radiated warmth through the cool air as he came down the steps and opened my car door. "You returned."

His green gaze was upon me, drinking me in and sending detonations to my nerve endings. With only his stare, he was doing things to me that I never knew were possible. Offering me his hand, I willingly placed my palm in his and stepped from the car. "Did you think I wouldn't return?"

Our touch lingered, sending warmth through my body despite the way our breath came out in vapor clouds in the coldness.

Van looked down at our hands and back to me. "Let me help you with your things and then we can pull your car into the garage. The weather forecast has more snow and plummeting temperatures coming overnight."

"Can they plummet more?" I asked, lifting my face to the falling snow, allowing the large flakes to land on my cheeks and eyelashes. The scene was so peaceful that I turned to Van. "I don't mind the snow or cold as long as I'm not stranded on the side of the road."

Am I concerned about Skylar's drive back to Chicago?
Does it make me a bad person that I'm not?

I didn't know the answer. I only knew I wanted to look forward and not backward.

Van laughed. "You took longer than I anticipated. I was beginning to get worried that I'd need to go searching for you."

"I made it."

He pulled me against him. "I would, Julia. I'd search the world for you. Now that I found you, I'd never allow you to be stranded again."

For a moment, I basked in his gaze, allowing the thrill of his touch to flow through me. Feeling his toned body against mine, I finally asked, "Is this part of the employee-and-employer agreement?"

"It's after-hours."

My gaze was glued to the way the golden flecks in his eyes glistened beneath the floodlights. "Maybe we should define this further. For example, here is work and" —I smiled— "how far away is the cabin?"

"A couple of miles," he said, releasing me. "First things first, your things."

An hour later, Van and I were seated at his kitchen table, eating dinner paired with a bottle of red wine. A fire roared in the large living-room fireplace and beyond the windows, the forecast snow was falling.

Van had explained how a woman he's known most of his life came once a week and cooked his meals. All he had to do was warm them up when he came home.

"This is delicious," I said, taking another bite of the chicken fettuccine Alfredo.

"Better than coffee and nectarines."

"The coffee was warm and those nectarines were fantastic. I was a little leery of the soup."

Van grinned. "The cans weren't that old. I like staying out at the cabin when I want to get away from everything. I keep the soup there for when my decision is impulsive. There's no cell service and being out there gives me a break."

Inhaling, I leaned back and lifted my face to the ceiling high above. "That's what being here is for me."

"I hate to tell you, but you do have cell service here and internet."

"I also have this nice button on the side of my phone that turns it off."

"Hmm. Maybe I should try that."

"You should. It's liberating." I took another sip of the wine. "I had a visitor in Ashland."

Van's expression changed as his chiseled jaw clenched. "A visitor?"

"Skylar was at the hotel."

"Had you told him where you were staying?"

I shook my head.

"Did you tell your parents or your assistant?"

"I didn't, but I suppose Leigh could look at the credit card account and figure it out."

"She's your assistant."

He hadn't asked, but I nodded.

"You came face-to-face with your *ex*" —he emphasized the syllable— "-fiancé and yet you're here with me."

"Seeing him didn't make me want to go back to him. I'm not ready to be with anyone. For the first time, I want to find out who I am, who I can be without the past, and most importantly" —I lifted the wine glass and smiled— "who I am when I'm with you."

"You're magnificent, that's who you are."

Warmth filled my cheeks at his comment. Taking another sip of wine, I sighed. "I like this. It's not too sweet or too dry."

As we finished our meal, Van stood, taking the plates to the sink. For a moment, I sat and watched. My father was a modern-day man in his thoughts and actions, yet my parents had a live-in cook and maid. I'd never seen my father, or Skylar for that matter, scrape a plate and put it in a dishwasher.

"I can help," I volunteered.

"I'm almost done." Van turned toward me, his gaze warming me from the inside. "I told you that I'm not used to giving tours of my home. I'm also not used to having a beautiful woman here. If you want to go up to your suite, I understand. If you're open to figuring out what after-hours means, I'd say we take the remaining wine out to the living room and talk."

I looked down at my dress pants and blouse. I'd left the heels in the suite. "I feel overdressed."

"You're stunning." He tugged on his flannel shirt. "Of course, I'd be willing to share."

It was unbelievable how much I wanted that. I wanted to strip down to my bra and panties and settle in wearing Van's shirt. I imagined the soft material and the scent of Van's cologne. The thoughts alone beaded my nipples.

"I'd like to talk."

"I'd like to do more than talk."

Chapter 13

Van

*L*ifting the bottle of wine, I knew that I was losing my battle with myself. The restraint I'd exercised throughout the day disappeared with the sunlight. Much like the wolves that came and went from my property, I had my prey in my sights and any self-control I'd forced myself to exhibit waned with each passing second. My hunger was growing to the point of starvation, and it wasn't food that I sought.

Julia walked beyond the sofa and fireplace to the windows and stared out toward the bay. "I can't describe how I feel right now." She spun toward me. "It's new."

I could stare at her for hours. Julia carried herself in a way that exhibited confidence and need at the same time. The dichotomy was fascinating. Her openness and honesty were inviting. It wasn't simply her beauty and her youth; Julia had a presence that lured me toward her.

"Tell me."

She shrugged. "It's consuming, you know, as they talk about in books. I didn't think the kind of attraction that they described was real. I've never been attracted to someone so much that everything else in life pales in importance."

Her admission made me smile. "You described it well." After setting the bottle of wine on the table between the sofa and fireplace, I took a step toward her. "I can describe what I see." I scanned from Julia's painted toenails to her beautiful yellow hair, no longer contained in a twist as it had been earlier in the day. Now it flowed over her slender shoulders creating a wavy veil.

Her lips parted and closed.

"You're stunning, Julia. There's no denying that. If Butler didn't tell you that a thousand times a day, he didn't truly see what a rare gift he wasted. The thing is, as gorgeous as you are, your beauty isn't your greatest asset. When I see you and I'm near you, I sense your energy, your vitality, and your genuineness. Those are rare qualities.

"I spend a lot of time alone, but I also spend time with business, here in Wisconsin and while traveling. The authenticity I sense in you is unique." Taking another step toward her, I reached for the stem of her glass and set it on a nearby table. "I could become addicted."

She inclined her chin, keeping her blue eyes fixed on me. "Van, right now, I'm not sure about who you think I am. I'm different when I'm with you."

"I can't imagine you any other way."

She lowered her forehead to my chest. "It's as if I've walked out of a cloud or a fog, one that's been over me for most of my life." She wrapped her arms around my torso. "This, right here, right now, it feels too good to be real. I'm scared that if I blink it'll be gone."

My arms wrapped around her.

She was right about the way it felt to have her here in my home and in my arms.

I lifted her chin until I was basking in her blue stare. "The only person who can make this end is you."

Her head shook. "I don't want it to end."

"And I don't want to talk."

"You said sex would be discussed."

I pulled her closer until her softness melded with my hardness. Before the other night in the cabin, it had been a while since I'd been intimate with a woman. The rare interactions I enjoyed were primarily mutually self-indulgent. The abstinence I endured was self-inflicted. Perhaps it was my penitence. Whatever the reason, Julia had awakened a part of me that I hadn't until recently realized had fallen into hibernation.

Her warm hand came to my cheek. "Red sin? Is that a real thing?"

"I haven't looked it up. I suppose it could be one of those sayings we hear and accept. Since I'd never experienced it, I was skeptical...until now. Now it feels real."

"It does."

I watched the way her lips moved.

The blue of her eyes swirled with emotions.

Julia should be afraid of the beast she'd awakened. Instead, she was pushing her petite body against mine and undoubtedly feeling my growing erection against her. She should run. I had to warn her. "Tell me good night. Don't let me blur the line of our agreement. Go up to your suite and lock the door."

"I don't want to." Her hand landed on my chest. "I'm open to blurring the line."

"Does that mean you're done discussing sex?"

"It means I want you to take me, Van. I can't explain this desire. I've never felt anything like this before. I'm still not looking for forever because for once I'm satisfied with the present."

Satisfied.

The concept was foreign to me.

It contradicted my need for more, bigger, and better.

I wasn't satisfied.

I wasn't satisfiable.

And currently, my state could be classified more accurately as insatiable.

As my thoughts filled with the possibilities before me, my breaths became shallower and my pulse kicked up a beat. Julia rose up on her tiptoes as her lips connected with mine. All day long as I'd contemplated the possibility that our evening could go in this direction, I'd told myself that if it did, I should be gentle and go slow.

Now, with Julia's body against mine, those sentiments were washed away by the flood of my speeding circulation. I wrapped Julia's long hair around my fingers as I fisted her golden tresses and tipped her head backward. Her moan filtered through the air as our kiss deepened. My tongue sought entrance as I unapologetically took what she offered.

When we separated, I asked, "Do you remember my rule?"

Julia nodded. "I invited. The rest is up to you." Her pink tongue darted to her swollen lips. "I'm not completely inexperienced, but I like letting you lead." Her breasts heaved as she took a deep breath. "I trust you."

My eyes briefly closed.

If she only knew how wrong she was.

With my cock achingly hard, I couldn't think about her misplaced trust. Now that her invitation was out in the air, I wouldn't back away.

I couldn't.

With the backdrop of the crackling fire, I made my proclamation, "Strip for me, beautiful."

As pink filled Julia's cheeks, I gently placed my hand on the side of her face. "I took your clothes off the other night. Now I want to watch as you take them off for me, knowing what's going to happen, knowing what I'm going to do to you."

Her blue orbs swirled with uncertainty. That was good. She should be uncertain.

"I don't know what you're going to do."

"Oh, I'm going to bury myself inside your perfect pussy."

She sucked in a breath as her eyes opened wider.

"And I'm not going to stop until we both come over and over."

As if the temperature had dropped, Julia began to tremble. I ran my finger down her cheek, to her neck, watching her pulsating carotid. I lowered my lips and kissed her neck, going lower and lower until I reached the top of her blouse. "I'm going to suck your nipples until they're hard as diamonds. I'm going to taste your sweet essence and dine on your juices."

"Van..."

I placed my finger on her lips. "Now, don't make me repeat myself. Strip for me."

She nodded as she looked around. "Everything is so open."

"And there isn't another person for miles. No one will see you or hear you scream as you come."

Her fingers slowly undid each button behind her neck. With her gaze fixed on mine, she lifted the blouse, exposing the lace bra beneath. Next, she unbuckled the skinny belt before undoing two buttons and the zipper to her slacks. Letting go of the waist, the slacks fell to the floor in a black puddle.

Beautiful blue eyes stayed fixed on me, staring up through her veiled lashes as she unclasped the bra.

I had plans for her perfect breasts; however, it was obvious by her reddened areolas and beaded nipples that she was already on her way. Next, she snagged the waist of the lace panties and pushed them to her ankles, stepping away from the pile of her clothing.

"Turn around slowly."

Julia was perfection, as if a master sculptor had created exactly what God intended.

Finders keepers.

I dropped the flannel shirt and pulled the thermal one over my head. I'd removed my boots earlier, making it too easy to unbuckle my belt and quickly lose my jeans to the floor. Still wearing my silk boxers straining to contain my erection, I offered Julia my hand. Her energy flowed through our touch as I walked her to the rug before the fireplace. I didn't say a word as she sat on the soft rug and lay back, lifting her arms over her head.

She was a fucking angel come to earth.

I didn't deserve her.

The calls I'd received warning me against marriage were right. The calls came from people who knew me. Julia didn't know me and yet here she was laid out, a beautiful vivacious gift that I would never tire of nor return.

In the light of the fire, lighter and darker shades of blond were visible in her hair. Such as the predator I was, I lowered myself to the rug and crawled over Julia until my lips were again claiming hers. Her hands came to my shoulders as her arms then wrapped around my neck.

Her kiss tasted like wine.

I prized myself away, letting my kisses rain lower, enjoying every inch of the flesh she offered me. Each nipple was licked, sucked, and nipped, leaving a peppering of goose bumps over her flesh. Her moans and whimpers superseded the crackling of the fire. I didn't stop as my tongue found her core. One lick and I knew she was wet and ready.

One lick and I wanted more.

Spreading her knees farther apart, I buried my face where soon my cock would be.

"Van."

She called out my name as her body writhed

beneath my ministrations. Swirling her clit, I inserted two fingers into her tight pussy, creating a rhythm as her hips bounced in time. By the way her legs tightened around my head, I knew she was close. I curled my fingers and nipped her clit. The room filled with her wordless sounds as she came undone in my grasp.

When her gaze met mine, a blushing smile filled her expression. "That was..."

"Just the beginning."

"I've never come that hard with oral."

Butler was a dick.

"Oh, there's more to come." I smiled. "Pun intended."

I stripped out of my boxer briefs and crawled back over her until our lips met. My tongue danced with hers. "See how good you taste?"

More pink came to her cheeks, giving her a glow in the fire's light.

Carefully, I guided my cock to her warm and wet heaven. With my elbows near her face, I stared down at Julia, taking in her youth, her beauty, and her trusting gaze. "Keep your eyes open, Julia. I want to watch you come this time. Don't look away."

Opening her eyes, she nodded.

With each inch, my hunger grew until I slammed deep inside her. Her squeal reverberated through the room, giving me pause. "I want you so badly."

"Don't stop."

I waited, giving her time to take me in. Even without moving, just having her tight walls contract around me was ecstasy.

She nodded as her lips met mine. "Take me. I want all of you."

It was her repeated invitation, and I wasn't going to turn her down. Pistoning my hips, I eased in and out, filling her with each thrust as she dug her fingernails into the rug's fibers and held on.

Her marvelous pussy, sensual noises, and expressions ranging from pain to bliss were feeding my hunger. Call me a chauvinist, but knowing that no one else had done this to her filled me with a cave-man-like need to keep her here and never let her go.

Julia's eyelids fluttered as she held on to my neck, our noses touching.

My balls grew tighter as I thrust faster, knowing she was again close and wanting to watch her display as she came.

It was as her body stiffened that I saw the splendor in her eyes.

That was the incentive I needed as I laid her shoulders back to the rug and lifted her bent legs to my shoulders. The sight before me was stunning. The end of my glistening cock was inside her wet pink pussy. Lifting her torso into my arms, I thrust upward.

"Oh, Van."

Fuck, it felt good.

In this position I was buried deeper than I'd been before.

Julia's youth and fitness allowed her the most satisfying flexibility. With her basically folded in half in my arms, my cock had the perfect angle as my hips pistoned with unabandoned need.

Harder and harder.

Faster and faster.

This was the definition of insatiable desire.

Her petite hands held tight to my neck as I continued recklessly staking my claim. It was as my orgasm built that she came again, her entire body trembling in my grasp. It had been so long since I'd engaged in sex fueled by pure desire that I'd forgotten the number-one rule of safety and precaution. As my seed pulsated out of me, filling her, I didn't care.

That caveman need wanted only one thing.

To never let Julia go.

Chapter 14

Julia

If men were supposed to reach their sexual peak at eighteen, I couldn't imagine what Van had been like then. After a marathon session of incredible line-blurring sex, including but not limited to the rug, the sofa—over the arm of the sofa to be more precise, against the large windows, and with me balanced on the dining room table, we claimed satiation and exhaustion. As I stood on wobbly knees with evidence of our evening activities on my skin, Van slipped on his boxer briefs and handed me his flannel shirt with the sexiest damn grin.

"I like you wearing that."

As I put my arms through the arm holes, I lingered, taking in the scent of his cologne and the softness of the material. "I like wearing it."

Reaching for my clothes, I felt the warmth in my cheeks. "So...I guess this is good night?"

"I'm a lot of bad things, Julia. Despite my parents'

faults, they raised a gentleman." He offered his arm. "May I escort you to your suite?"

Giggling softly, I placed my hand in the crook of his bent arm. "You are a gentleman, Mr. Sherman."

"I'm not," he said, as we ascended the staircase, "but I know how to act like one."

When we entered the sitting room of my suite, I tossed my clothes onto a chair. "Thank you for the escort."

His green orbs glistened with the desire from earlier. "If I stay in here, that blurred line will cease to exist."

"I believe after the dining room table, the line completely disappeared." My gaze met his. "Did we clean the table?"

He laughed. "Yes."

"I guess I was preoccupied."

Honestly, I wasn't certain that I could physically handle more of what we'd done. My body was sore and worn out in the best of ways. I lifted myself up on my tiptoes and gave him a kiss. "We can talk about the line, if it still exists, in the morning." I turned to go into the bathroom. Before I shut the door, I said, "Good night, Van."

This was my way of not being clingy. I wasn't in the market for forever. Walking away, even to the bathroom, gave Van an out without either of us feeling abandoned.

After taking care of business, cleaning myself, brushing my teeth and hair, and deciding to keep Van's shirt as my nightgown, I opened the door. The sitting room was empty. Van was gone.

I stood for a moment, contemplating his departure. There was nothing to overthink. I'd offered him the door, he took it. Besides, if we were to maintain any form of line, he'd made the right move.

Turning off the lights, I made it back to the large bedroom when I heard a knock.

'There are no people for miles...'

His words from earlier left little confusion regarding who was at the door to my suite.

When I opened the door, Van was standing with one arm on the doorjamb, looking sexy with his messy hair, five o'clock shadow, no shirt, and low-hanging blue jeans. "Yes?"

"You forgot this." He pulled my bra from behind his back.

A smile came to my lips. "Oops." I retrieved my bra.

"I thought you might not want to leave it out for Margaret to find."

"Who's Margaret?"

"She's Mrs. Mayhand's daughter."

I was trying to remember. "The woman who cooks?"

"Yes. She and Margaret come here every Friday morning. That's tomorrow."

"Will she make it through the snow?"

"It's stopped. Margaret's husband will be here in a few hours to plow my lane. I usually leave for the office before seven." Van looked down at his shirt that I was wearing and back to me. "I wanted you to know because even though no one heard or saw us tonight, tomorrow, if you decide to go to the kitchen dressed as you are, you may run into Mrs. Mayhand or Margaret."

I crossed my arms over my chest. "I'm glad you told me."

The clock on the bookcase said that it was nearly one in the morning. "Do you care if they know I'm here?"

"They know."

I stood taller. "They do?"

"Not who you are but that I have a houseguest."

"You'll be gone?" I contemplated meeting these people without Van present. If I were to stay for a while, Fridays would come and go. Tomorrow, or today, was as good of a time as any. "I'll be fully dressed before leaving the suite."

Van's devilish grin returned. "As your employer, I am considering a dress code, a uniform."

Heat returned to my tired body. "We can discuss that and the invisible line tomorrow."

Van took a step closer, crossing the threshold and reaching for my face. "I have meetings tomorrow and am overbooked because of meetings I canceled for today." He kissed my lips. "Never have I wanted to play hooky this badly."

I reached for his hand. "Did you turn off all the lights?"

"The house is secure, if that's what you're asking."

My focus went to where our hands were connected. "Mr. Sherman, do you cuddle?"

His eyes opened wide at my question. "Do I *cuddle*?"

The answer seemed obvious in his surprised expression and the emphasis he'd placed on the word, yet I pushed. "Yes, do you cuddle or are you a wham-bam-thank-you-ma'am type of man?"

"Of late, I'm mostly neither. Historically, I would say wham-bam."

I tugged his hand toward the bedroom. "Tonight, you'll cuddle."

"Remember my rule."

"I do. When it comes to sex, you lead the way. Tonight, you led the way many times. Now this isn't sex. It isn't even an invitation for more." We were in the bedroom. "This is sleeping and cuddling."

His skeptical expression morphed. "I'm not declining your invitation. However, if I wake and your sexy body is there, I can't promise cuddling won't become sex."

I pulled back the covers on the far side of the bed and walked around to the nearer side and did the same. Sitting on the edge of the bed, I assessed the man staring at me. "Maybe instead of never enough, your memoir should be about your inability to respect boundaries."

"I respect them, Julia. I see them as challenges."

"Challenges you must overcome."

"Every challenge must be overcome."

"Turn off the light, Van. I want to go to sleep and since our employer-employee line has been obliterated, I want to cuddle. Come cuddle."

He didn't argue as he turned off the light and climbed into the big bed beside me. The king-size bed was larger than the one in the cabin. We both moved toward the middle. "Thank you," I said as I settled next to him. With my leg near his, I knew he'd taken off the blue jeans and was back to his boxer briefs.

"Good night, Julia."

"Good night." I fell asleep tucked in the fold of his strong arm, with my head on his chest as his heart thumped a lullaby.

I woke to an empty bed and soreness in muscles that until recently I hadn't known existed. Stretching on the soft sheets, I rolled to where Van had slept.

With my head on his pillow, I inhaled, smelling his cologne. Beyond the windows, the sun shone, reflecting off the snow. Closing my eyes, I recalled last night.

The dining room table had been an incredible experience. With me perched on the edge, my knees bent, and my feet on the table at my sides, I had a ringside view of our bodies coming together.

I'd gone from never having sex to being fascinated by the sight of Van's large cock moving in and out of me. He was both thick and long, thicker than Skylar. I wasn't completely inexperienced; I'd seen an erect penis before. While Skylar and I never had intercourse, we'd done petting and oral.

This was different. Seeing the stretched skin and veins all covered in our come and glistening under the dining room chandelier as Van moved in and out of me was satisfying and unbelievable at the same time. It would seem that the physics of what was happening was impossible; he was too big or I was too small, and yet we fit perfectly.

Maybe the visual was why some people liked porn. It was one of the many things I'd never done— watched porn. But in my mind, what we'd done was different. I hadn't watched two strangers or two actors. I was there, seeing our connection, hearing the noises we made, feeling his girth as he filled me, smelling his skin against mine, and tasting his kisses.

I couldn't have prized myself away.

Even remembering the scene had my tired muscles clenching at nothing.

The clock on the bedside said it was after nine. That meant that Van was at his office and there could be two women I didn't know downstairs. If they knew I was here, they probably thought I was hiding.

The truth was that I had slept a blissful sleep in Van's arms.

Unlike in the cabin, this time the air beyond the bed wasn't frigid.

In the bathroom, I unbuttoned his shirt. As I did, standing before the large mirror over the vanity, I saw red and pink splotches were visible on my neck and breasts. While I'd felt the coarseness of Van's whiskers and enjoyed how they teased my sensitive skin, I hadn't realized that they'd left their marks. I looked closer. My eyes opened wide, followed by my gaping mouth.

I had a hickey.

Oh my God, I hadn't had a hickey since...I couldn't remember.

Has Skylar ever given me a hickey?

I couldn't recall. Gently, I palpated the skin as my smile bloomed. Being that the small bruise was on my breast, it would be easy to hide.

Am I crazy that I'm not angry that Van has left behind a mark?

Should I be upset?

I wasn't at all.

Yes, our line had been blurred to the point of obliteration. And yet, as I stepped under the warm water within the glass shower, I had no regrets.

I was an adult woman who made a choice on her own, based on her own desires. Regret was the farthest thought from my mind as I washed my hair and gently washed my body. Being here, just outside Ashland, in Van's large house was where I wanted to be.

Today was Friday.

I'd walked out on my forever a week ago. Last Friday night was when I'd left my engagement ring on the counter. It was the last time I'd spoken to my best friend. I contemplated the timeline, following the white ribbon and spending time in Ashland before the interview.

The days blurred, just like Van's and my line.

Thoughts of the canceled wedding came like lead weights pulling me down into the depths of the Great Lake. I imagined the wedding dress my mother and I had selected—another weight. The large venue, flowers, and decorations—more weights. The guest list—hundreds more. My forced smile as I took my vows—the anchor was large enough to keep an ocean liner from moving.

I hadn't even realized how close I'd been to drowning.

Now, instead of sinking, for the first time, I spread my wings and flew, soaring through the cobalt blue sky. Possibilities I never imagined were before me. Feelings I never realized I was missing were coursing through me.

Van's and my attraction was new and exciting.

Surely with time it would fade.

It wasn't as if we'd have marathon sex sessions every night forever.

Besides, I wasn't looking for forever.

With my hair dried and secured in a low ponytail, minimal makeup, and wearing a long sweater, soft stretch pants, and warm socks, all covering any marks Van had left behind, I reached for my laptop bag. As I did, I saw the note.

Julia,

There's no rush. Feel free to relax all day. After all, you (and I) were rather active last night. I'm not sorry I woke you. You're so damn responsive, I couldn't help myself.

Warmth crept up my cheeks.

I had thought that was a dream. Unlike the other times, during the night, our middle-of-the-night connection was slow and sweet, the lovemaking phase after the fucking. The memories returned as I'd held on to him as we both reached our peaks and floated back to earth.

I continued to read:

The information I promised you to use to write the memoir is now in the library. Feel free to make that room your study or office. I'll try to be home at a decent hour. After all, we have a line to erase, or was it discuss?

I can't recall. I'm having trouble concentrating on this note with you in the next room.

Have a good day,

Van

I picked up the laptop bag and stuffed his note inside. Opening the door of the suite, I was off to find a late breakfast and the library. Maybe Mrs. Mayhand or Margaret could help.

Chapter 15

Van

*M*y thoughts continually circled back to the beautiful woman I'd found in the freezing snowstorm. I wasn't a man who saved people or did anything without the promise of reciprocation. That knowledge alone had me questioning myself and my motives.

What do I want?

Do I want to keep Julia?

Do I want her to see me as others don't, as someone who saves instead of destroys?

Or is the attention I've given to Wade Pharmaceutical not about Julia McGrath but because of her?

She'd brought the vulnerability of Wade and of Marlin Butler back into my sights.

Speaking of Butler, I'd had my private eye do a run of Skylar Butler's credit cards. His last charge was at a gas station in Madison around ten thirty last night. I couldn't help but compare our dissimilar situations. He'd been pumping gas, and I'd been pumping my cock in and out of Julia.

It was thoughts like those that brought a smile to my lips.

I was between meetings with my concentration on the information on my computer screen.

The fifteen percent of Wade Pharmaceutical stock not owned by McGrath, Butler, or me was distributed between eight entities. That meant one of two things.

One, the investment was considered so low and unsubstantial that the owners wouldn't panic sell.

Or two, the investment was so low and unsubstantial that they'd jump at the chance to sell, especially at a price higher than the environment demanded.

The ring of my phone pulled my thoughts away from the list of Wade stockholders. The entities and names were unfamiliar, but I'd have my people do some digging. Even privately held stock was public record.

Picking up the telephone receiver, I clenched my jaw as Connie announced the caller, Lena Montgomery. I wasn't surprised that she'd called my office. A part of me wanted to be irritated. After all, I'd avoided Lena's calls for the last twenty-four hours. A larger part of me was impressed with her diligence.

I knew Lena too well to think that she'd simply give up.

"Put her through," I told Connie. I waited as the lines connected.

"Van." My shortened name rolled off Lena's sugar-coated tongue. "Nice of you to take my call."

My lips curled at the confection-filled bitchiness of her tone.

Lena Montgomery was the kind of woman who would smile her brightly painted lips, bat her lush long lashes, and distract men and women with her combination of class, curves, and deceptions. And then she'd take what she wanted. Hell, sometimes they willingly handed it to her.

In the world of wolves, we'd found one another.

"I thought it was," I replied. "You know how I like to be considered nice."

"No need to worry. I won't tell a soul."

"Your secrets are safe with me, too."

She hummed. "Maybe your cell phone isn't working."

"No, Lena, it's working. I've been busy." My thoughts returned to Julia, who I'd left under the blankets wearing nothing but my shirt.

"I should have said I was too busy to help when you called."

She was right to point out that she hadn't.

Lena continued, "I've spoken to Jeremy. He said you were able to secure the stock."

I leaned back against my chair, turning away from my desk and the large computer screens and toward the tall windows. The tempered glass lessened the sun's reflection on the white paradise. Some people would detest the frozen scene before me. I didn't. I appreciated the isolation brought on by Mother Nature. "That is correct. Thank you, Ms. Montgomery. Your help was priceless."

"Oh, come on, you know nothing is priceless."

"Everything has a price."

"And every*one*," she added. "I've been racking my brain since you called the other night, trying to figure out your endgame. Now that you have the stock, tell me what you have planned. I know you hate Marlin Butler as much as I do, but damn, you just paid too much for a company that's bound to end up as a footnote on a pharmaceutical giant's portfolio. I've done some follow-up and with Marlin's son's—Skylar's—fiancée taking off before their wedding, the value of Wade has begun to tank. Is watching Butler falter not good enough for you?"

"Lena, you know me better than that. Having Butler fail isn't enough. It never will be enough. Was it enough for you when you fucked Logan?"

Logan was Marlin's brother.

For the record, I intended for the verb to have multiple meanings.

Lena's story was complicated. Her parents died tragically in an accident that netted her and her sister a handsome payout. She ended up in a relationship with a divorced attorney who offered to help turn their settlement into more. He did make it more, just not for her or her sister.

At that point, the two of us had yet to meet.

Finding herself in need of financial help, Lena agreed to a one-year assignment. It covered her housing and food and paid exceptionally well, allowing her to help her sister. The company was by referral only and was headquartered in New York. When she signed the contract, Lena agreed to be available to the person who held her contract for the year. It was explicitly explained that while sex was implied, this wasn't a sexual agreement and being that she came from a good family, everything was confidential.

Nearly twenty years ago, Lena was paired with a man who was planted as a decoy by Logan Butler, the same attorney who took her money. The arrangement settled a debt for that man. It also landed Logan, the man who stole her and her sister's future, back in Lena's life.

Not long after she signed the contract, the two of us met, introduced by Lena's sister.

My friendship with Lena was conceived by a mutual desire to bring down Logan and the company that imprisoned her for a year, Infidelity. Once we were done, so was Infidelity. No one else would be subjected to what Lena had been. Our actions weren't pure or selfless in intent. We both walked away with a sizeable payday. A company like Infidelity will pay an exorbitant amount to keep its clients' names safe.

Lena's voice brought me back to present. "Logan Butler fucked up when he thought he could take what wasn't his and then turn around and continue to control me."

In my mind's eye, I could see Lena's smile and the shimmer of her brown eyes. "And Marlin came to his rescue, one of his many mistakes."

Her laugh rang through the receiver. "I don't mind helping you take down Marlin. Tell me why there's such a rush."

Inhaling, I debated telling my old friend about Julia McGrath. Call me selfish, but for a short time, I wanted to keep Julia to myself.

"Van?"

"As you mentioned, Wade Pharmaceutical has been vulnerable. I can list three different larger pharmaceutical companies, including two of the ones currently reaping the benefit of large government contracts, that are willing to swallow up Wade. Jeremy confirmed my suspicion that Marlin Butler was ready to buy additional stock. He'd already laid the groundwork with the shareholders, finding the ones willing to sell. If Butler would have carried out his plan, Marlin would be a few shares away from owning the majority of Wade, even without his son's marriage."

"I read that the two are working on reconciliation. Maybe Marlin wants his cake and to eat it too."

I was certain that Julia wasn't currently working on reconciliation with Skylar Butler, but I couldn't share that without giving up my secret.

Lena continued "It doesn't sound like Butler's goal is to make Wade stronger."

A grin came to my face. "Hell no. He's been waiting to sell. Selling after the wedding would put Wade at a high. Marlin Butler would've cashed out and tripled the worth of each share."

"So your rush to purchase wasn't about owning Wade's private stock but about stopping Butler from cashing in."

"Now, I need to get Butler's stock," I said.

"Why do you want a tiny pharmaceutical company located in the Midwest?"

"Maybe I want to be philanthropic and provide low-cost medication to the masses."

"Right," Lena said, "your philanthropic desires have always dictated your financial moves. Besides, you know, Butler's portfolio includes more than his shares of Wade. He's diversified. If Wade drops in value as I anticipate, he'll dump it."

That gave me another thought. "There's the issue with him being one of the original stockholders when Herman Wade offered stock to new investors."

"If you're insinuating that Marlin Butler will go down with the ship out of some sense of loyalty, your recent desire to help the masses has clouded your judgment."

"I don't just want his Wade stock, Lena, I want everything. I want to watch him standing on the bow of that sinking ship as it slips into the depths of Lake Superior."

"I hear it's cold."

"Not where he's going."

Marlin Butler's most recent sin was his plan to screw Julia. The nail in his coffin was Julia's and my meeting. Yes, he'd been on my radar, but now that radar was laser focused.

My mind went to Julia and to her parents. I didn't know them. My knowledge was coming in slowly. What little I'd learned in the last forty-eight hours gave me the feeling that Gregg McGrath had worked hard over the last decade, perhaps out of a sense of duty to his wife's family, working to keep Wade liquid and profitable. I had a private detective digging for more information.

The McGraths weren't big contenders in the

financial world or even in the world of pharmaceuticals. Wade's claim to fame began with one of the first patents of insulin. Julia's grandfather made his mistake by putting too much time and money into fighting generic distribution. Instead of fighting, he should have jumped onboard, accepting the fate of generics and profiting from both sides.

"Marlin Butler is close with Gregg McGrath," I said, "even though he was planning on screwing him."

"It's always easiest to screw those closest to you."

She was right.

Lena sighed. "I'm going to ask one more time. Why are you, Donovan Sherman, devoting time to this small company?"

"I have an interest."

"Beyond Butler?"

"I have a callout to Jeremy." Jeremy was a talented and gifted wizard when it came to anything regarding market irregularities. "He's watching Marlin Butler for me. If his private stocks go into the sale mode, I'll know. Jeremy knows that I want them."

"If you have a want list for Jeremy, you should answer my calls."

If the world were divided up into the people on my side and those on Lena's side, Jeremy was hers. She'd found him first. Lena had helped make Jeremy a very wealthy man. His talents have done the same for her. Of course, she has other assets and abilities that have also added to her bottom line.

Lena and Jeremy also shared other mutual interests.

Lena and I had explored those interests too.

We were better as allies with a common enemy than we were in other roles.

"You know how cell service can be up here," I said in the way of an excuse.

Lena's voice sweetened. "Of course you can use Jeremy, just be open with me."

"I am."

"Shall we discuss Madison...?"

She had my attention. "Let me call you back from my cell."

"Yes, Van, let's chat."

I wasn't certain how much I'd disclose. Lena knew my secrets better than anyone. I knew hers too. Now I needed to at least make her think she was in on my plan.

Julia

$\mathcal{W}$alking down the stairs, I heard the sound of a vacuum before I came to the bottom step and face-to-face with a woman I assumed was Margaret, the lady who Van had mentioned. Wearing blue jeans and a sweatshirt, she was moving about the tile and wood floors with a pull-behind vacuum. Although she had some signs of age, such as a few wrinkles, with her short blond hair, fit figure, and abounding energy, I didn't think she was the mother in this duo.

As soon as she saw me, a large smile blossomed across the woman's face. "Hello, Donovan said he had a guest."

I offered her my hand. "That would be me. I'm Julia."

"Hi, Julia. I'm Margaret, and my mother, Paula, is in the kitchen. If you're hungry she can make you something."

Her friendly greeting left me with a smile. "Oh, that's not necessary. I can find something."

Margaret lowered her voice. "I don't know how long you're visiting, Julia, but here's a bit of advice from me to you. When it comes to my mother, it's her mission in life to feed everyone. She bakes cookies for the mailman, takes cakes to doctors' offices, donates to animal shelters, volunteers at homeless food kitchens—"

"And supplies a week's meals to Donovan," I interrupted, using the name Margaret had used for Van.

"I know it may not seem like he's as helpless as the dogs, cats, and homeless, but he is."

That made me smile. So far, I didn't see Van as helpless in any way, but our interactions had not included cooking and cleaning. "Are you saying that it would be a hopeless cause for me to refuse your mother's cooking?"

Margaret nodded. She tilted her head as she took me in. "I'm sorry. You look familiar. If you don't mind me asking, are you Donovan's sister?"

His sister.

I didn't know if he had a sister. Then again, I knew very little about the man.

My lips came together. "No, no relation."

"Oh." Her eyes widened. "Oh."

I shook my head with a smile. "It's nice to meet you, Margaret."

"You too, Julia."

The open floor plan glistened with a fresh shine and the generous amount of sunshine coming through the large windows. The frozen bay caught my attention. The snowdrifts glistened like motionless waves from yesterday's wind. Soft white clouds floated in a blue sky above the horizon. As I turned around in the living room, I was bombarded with the memories of last night. I quickly spun back to the windows, fearful we'd left clues of our night's line-erasing on the glass pane.

I took a step one direction and then the other, tilting my head to see from different angles. A sigh of relief came at the cleanliness of the window.

"Strange smudge," Margaret said, coming up behind me.

I spun toward her. "Excuse me."

Warmth came from my toes, radiating toward my neck and cheeks.

The tips of her lips curled in a friendly way. She shook her head. "Very unusual," she said. "Rarely are Donovan's windows in need of cleaning on the inside, just normal dust and air particles. This morning there was a rather large smudge right in the area where you are looking." She shrugged. "The good news is it cleaned with no issues."

I took a deep breath. "That is good news."

"Enjoy some breakfast."

I nodded, walking through the dining room on my way to the kitchen. A quick inspection of the table let me know that it was clean. I could only hope that it had been cleaned by Van as he'd said, not Margaret.

If she knew the cause of the smudge, she also knew I wasn't Van's sister.

Why do I look familiar?

Before I could give that more thought, my stomach growled at the delicious aromas filling the air.

The six-burner stove was filled with pots and pans as a petite older woman with dark black hair tended to each one. Such as her daughter, this woman also wore blue jeans and flat white tennis shoes. Instead of a sweatshirt, she had on a plain black top with a long black sweater over the top. Around her waist was an apron, reminding me of the ones my grandmother would wear when we baked cookies or she let me help her with something.

"Hello," I called out over the sounds of bubbling and simmering pots.

Mrs. Mayhand, or Paula, quickly turned. Wiping her hands on her apron, she scanned me up and down. There was a moment of contemplation on her part before she smiled. "Hello. So you're Mr. Sherman's guest."

"I am. My name is Julia."

She nodded. "My name is Paula. Most people call me Mrs. Mayhand." She winked. "I think it's because they think I'm old. I'm not too old to remember my first name."

I grinned. "It's nice to meet you, Paula."

Her smile broadened. "And you too. What may I get you for" —she looked at the clock— "lunch or is this breakfast?"

Technically, it was somewhere in between. "We could call it brunch."

Paula walked to a far counter, pulled a coffee mug from a peg. "I have a pot of coffee over here. It's my indulgence while I cook. Would you like a cup?"

I laid my computer bag on the kitchen table and walked to the breakfast bar "I don't mind serving myself."

"I'm only here one day a week. Let an old lady have her way."

Nodding, I sat up on the high stool. "Yes, please. Coffee would be great."

"Cream or sugar?"

"Cream, if you have it."

Paula opened the refrigerator and shook her head. "Is black all right? You tell me some things you like and I'll add them to the list." She handed me the warm black coffee.

"I really don't know how long I'll be staying."

As I spoke, she wrote cream on a long list.

"What are you cooking?"

"Mr. Sherman isn't much for celebrating holidays. You might have chosen a bad time to visit."

I looked around the large kitchen and out to the living room. "I hadn't given his lack of decorations much thought."

"Oh, no, he doesn't decorate."

"I can see how it would be a lot of work for only one person to enjoy."

Paula checked on her pans before pushing a light on the double oven and looking inside. She smiled and turned my way. "When Peggy told me that Mr. Sherman had a guest, I decided he needed a holiday meal." She shrugged. "He may not like it, but I have a turkey breast in the oven, gravy on the stove and two different casseroles and mashed potatoes already in the refrigerator. I'll write out warming instructions. No sense in two people spending the holiday without plenty to eat."

"It sounds delicious."

"Now, about your brunch."

"Is there fruit?" I asked.

"Oh, yes. Mr. Sherman likes his nectarines."

I lifted my coffee mug to my lips, trying to hide my smile. "Nectarines and coffee sounds perfect."

"Let me make you an English muffin." She looked at me. "Or are you one of those no-carbs people."

"I'm one of those too-many-carbs people."

I think that won me a few brownie points as Paula grinned and nodded. Soon I was feasting on nectarines, an English muffin drenched in real butter, and coffee. I was also answering Paula's detailed questions about my eating preferences.

"As I said, I'm not sure how long I'll be here."

"Oh, child, you're changing up my cooking routine, and I couldn't be more grateful. Mr. Sherman is a creature of habit. I make six meals each week. The next week, I clean out the refrigerator of all the leftovers he didn't eat. I can almost guarantee which meals will be gone and which will be only partially eaten. Every week, I rotate the menu. If I throw in something new, I'll find it untouched the next week. I love cooking; I'm even more thrilled to mix it up a bit." She grinned my way. "Is that why you're here? To mix it up."

My muffin and fruit were gone. Apparently, I'd worked up an appetite last night. "I'm here because Mr. Sherman advertised for someone to write his memoir. I accepted the job."

Her lips came together as she nodded. "He wants someone to write his story?"

"Yes. I mean, he's an accomplished businessman from what I've read so far."

"I see—a book about his business feats. I suppose there would be people wanting to read about how he has done all he has accomplished."

"Sometimes these memoirs are more self-indulgent," I said. "It's more for the subject to get the satisfaction from telling their story."

Paula was back to the stove. "He isn't like that."

"What do you mean?"

She adjusted the heat on a few of the burners and turned my way. "I suppose that's for you to learn. No need to have your version of Mr. Sherman's story tainted by an old woman's observations."

"How long have you known Donovan?"

"Long enough to know he's a private man and it just doesn't seem right that he would want to tell the world his secrets."

"He has secrets?" I asked.

"Everyone has secrets. I suppose he wants this to be about Sherman and Madison Corporation. That would make sense."

The more we spoke, the more curious I was to dive into the information Van had compiled for this memoir. "Did his business begin down in Madison?"

Paula shook her head. "Started right here."

"Is Madison a family name, maybe his mother's family name?"

"Sometimes there are questions that are better left unasked."

I finished my coffee and lifted the mug and plate. Before I could go any farther, Paula shook her head. "Let me do that, Julia. Peggy and I will be out of here by three. If you need anything at all before then, don't hesitate to ask. And" —she pointed at her list— "you think of anything else you'd like from the store or for me to prepare, be sure to tell me."

"There is one thing."

"What is it?"

"Well, yesterday, Donovan gave me a quick tour. He said for me to set up an office in his library." I smiled at the ridiculousness of my question. "Could you point me toward the library?"

Chapter 17

Julia

The library that Van had offered as my home base, office, work center or whatever I wanted to call it was as stunning as the rest of his house. It was also cozier. I realized that there was beauty to the open concept, but four walls, two lined from floor to ceiling with books on beautiful wood bookcases, another with large domed windows looking out onto tall trees in a forest, and a fourth with the French door entry—not unlike the one at the front of the house—and another fireplace made me feel less exposed. The furniture was rich and sturdy. The desk was tall and wide, reminding me of the antique library tables.

I had barely dived into the information Van had accumulated as I got myself settled. He had plastic totes filled with physical information, magazines, newspapers, and photographs. After a quick search, I found the photos were primarily of buildings rather than people. There was also a file filled with flash drives in dated compartments.

This was what Van wanted in his memoir. I couldn't help but wonder what he didn't want in it and why. If I were simply a person from the outside hired to write his story, I didn't know if I'd have the same level of curiosity.

As it turned out, I wasn't simply an outsider, not anymore. Van had offered to marry me, for us to join in name as well as physically. That gave me the right to dig beyond the benign surface.

That's what I told myself.

More than once, Margaret came in to check on me. She also asked if she could clean my suite. I declined. While Van had warned me about coming downstairs dressed, he forgot to mention that someone may go into my suite, see my unmade bed, and draw the uncomfortable— albeit accurate— conclusion that I hadn't slept alone.

I couldn't get a good read on how I felt about Margaret and Paula or what they thought of me, but I did make a mental note to make my bed and pick up in my suite from today forward to any Fridays that followed.

I also replayed my conversation with Paula in my head, looking for answers to the myriad of questions forming, their number increasing by the minute. Van's last name was Sherman. Where did the 'Madison' come from in Sherman and Madison Corporation?

Why did Mrs. Mayhand say that some questions are better unasked?

Is there significance in his company's name that I don't know?

As my computer booted up and ran yet another update, I gave up on the totes and walked around the room, taking in this personal side of Donovan Sherman. Saying the room had four walls shouldn't imply that the library was small. It was a large square and also tall, the ceiling went up beyond the one in the hallway. If I had to guess, I'd say it went up two stories. The sliding ladder on the bookshelves was directly out of every little girl's dreams, any little girl who watched Belle dance and sing on a similar ladder.

The more I looked around, the more I became aware of what Van was lacking. While I hadn't been in every room in his home, not even close, I'd yet to see anything that resembled personal mementos. There were no framed pictures or special items.

Back at my family home, my mother's fireplace mantel was filled with pictures of our family, my grandparents and great-grandparents, my aunts and uncles, and my cousins. There were pictures dating back to before I was born. In Dad and Mom's home office was a large framed picture of William and Pricilla Wade. William was my mother's grandfather and the man who founded Wade Pharmaceutical. I never knew him. I knew my grandfather, William's son and my mother's father, Herman Wade. He was the person who ultimately decided to offer investment in Wade Pharmaceutical, diluting my family's influence in the operation of the privately held corporation. I knew from my study at Northwestern that the goal had been to raise capital.

According to my father, it was the wrong move. My grandfather had the ultimate power to make the decision. His plan was to limit investors to trusted friends who could bring an influx of funds and avoid debt in the difficult environment. My grandfather's decision went against my father's advice. The rift that ensued between my father and my mother's father was why our family's stock shares were headed to me upon my marriage. It was one of Grandfather Herman's blows to my father before Herman's death.

So far, I'd yet to see any pictures of Van's family.

That thought reminded me of Margaret's comment, asking if I was Van's sister.

With my laptop connected to the internet, my plan was to do more of a search on Donovan Sherman. Before I did, I scanned my emails and shook my head. The executive-in-training position I'd had for the last year at Wade accounted for ninety percent of my unopened emails. There a few from the wedding planner.

Mother could take care of anything regarding the wedding.

I typed out a request to Leigh, my assistant, telling her that I would be unreachable through at least the third of January—the end of the holiday weekend. I asked her to handle whatever arose and if she needed further direction to contact my mother or father.

When the rift between Grandfather Herman and Dad came to a head, Mom took her place in the company. She'd always been involved beneath the surface. However, the upheaval within the family was getting to be more than she could handle from afar. Today, both of my parents were co-CEOs.

Securing Mother's position was another of Grandfather's doings and a slap in the face to my father. Thankfully, my parents had worked it out. Grandfather might be disappointed if he knew how well my parents worked together.

One particular email heading caught my eye. It was dated last Saturday morning—the date I left Chicago. Subject line: Emergency meeting of shareholders. The email was sent by Marlin Butler.

I searched for the minutes from the meeting, but they weren't in my email.

Either the meeting was never called or I'd been omitted from receiving the minutes. Either way, my suspicion was piqued. I sent another message to

Leigh, asking for a follow-up on the meeting if there had been one. As I was about to log out of my email, another subject heading dated yesterday drew my attention. Unlike the company-wide email, this was directly from my father to me.

My finger lingered over the mouse, deciding whether I wanted to open, leave as unread, or delete.

I hadn't spoken to my father since I'd called off the wedding, only my mother.

Holding my breath, I opened the email. On the screen was the place to enter a pin.

This formality made me smile. The encoded email was something between me and my father.

We started our secret system when I was still in high school. We'd use our clandestine messages to plan surprises for my mother or to invite one another on special father-daughter dates. As an only child, I loved the times I'd get one parent to themselves. I'd dress up and Dad would take me to one of the restaurants downtown. Sometimes my mother and I would dress up and go to tea at the Drake Hotel.

The encoded lock on the email made it impossible for anyone else to come upon our correspondence and access what was written.

I entered the four numbers that were special to us.

The email opened.

. . .

Julia,

Please call me. I want to talk to my little girl.
Dad

"I'm not a little girl," I whispered, but his reference didn't upset me. It added to my guilt. Maybe I'd been selfish. Maybe my father would have more understanding for my situation. Then again, he was Marlin Butler's best friend, or he thought he was. If I called, I could warn him.

I took a deep breath as I looked at my phone. The signal was currently good with five bars and the battery charged.

Leaving both the information Van had left me and my laptop in the library, I stepped out into the main level. In the distance, I heard sounds as well as pots and pans and smelled the aromas of more and different foods. As I climbed the steps, I heard Margaret's vacuum in what I'd been told was Van's suite.

Curiosity pulled me toward her.

I made it to the hallway. Unlike the one containing my suite, there was only one option in this hallway, double doors at the end, currently ajar. All I'd have to do was take a few more steps to be at the threshold.

It was as if there was an invisible tug-of-war

occurring in the realm beyond my ability to see. I was pulled toward the doorway, hoping for more personal touches to Van's life and history. Surely a man as passionate as Van Sherman had mementos to remind him of others. And at the same time, there was a wall. It wasn't as if I could touch it, but it was there none-theless. It was a barrier that I didn't want to cross.

It was as if I were on a precipice.

Will I learn more about the man I am attracted to or will I lose his trust?

Chapter 18

Julia

One more step toward his suite and I changed my mind, quickly redirecting my destination. I'd enter Van's suite if and when he invited me. Van had opened his home to me. I wasn't going to snoop where I wasn't invited.

For some reason, as I passed the other door in the hallway to my suite, I twisted the handle. It didn't move. The door was locked. A locked door was not an invitation. When I stepped through the threshold to my suite, I found all the rooms exactly as I'd left them. My clothes from last night were still strewn on a chair in the sitting room. The large bed was unmade. The towel from my shower was hanging haphazardly from the towel bar.

It wasn't my lack of tidiness that made me smile but that Margaret respected my wishes—the boundary that I'd set. At least one person in my new life could do that.

Sitting in a large chair near the fireplace, I pulled

my feet up into the chair, wrapped one arm around my knees, and touched the screen, calling my father's private phone. The sound of a ring was quickly replaced with my father's voice.

"Julia, tell me this is you."

The desperation in his tone added to my newfound remorse at not calling him earlier. "It's me, Dad. I've spoken to Mom. Didn't she tell you?"

"Where are you?"

"I took a job in Ashland."

The noise behind Dad's voice went away as if he'd left a busy room. He didn't address my answer, instead asking more questions. "Have you looked at your emails? Tell me you care. Tell me you're not simply hiding when you could help."

I put my sock-covered feet back on the large rug and paced back and forth before the fireplace, my stomach twisting with each step. I hadn't read the emails. Each turn had me facing the beautiful snow-ladened bay and then away. "Dad, I'm not caught up. What's happening?"

He let out an exasperated sigh. "In the last week, the perceived value of Wade has dropped."

"I'm sorry. I've been a bit preoccupied by what happened with Skylar and now with me."

"Julia, you must come home. Christmas is in two days. Come home and let me explain what has happened since you left."

"What does it matter what the perceived value of Wade Pharmaceutical is? There is real value."

"Julia, we haven't been as forthcoming as we should, given you're about to be more involved. The truth is that Wade has been having financial problems during the last few years. We've relied on loans to keep us going. The banks allowed us to borrow and borrow some more because the bank officials believed we could pay it back. With the new belief that we're sinking, the largest loan has called a balloon payment due by January 3rd. Our options are to make the payment or accept an astronomical increase in interest."

"How would combining McGrath stock with Butler have stopped that?" I asked, trying to understand.

"That union was a show of strength. Now, it's even worse. We're under attack."

"What do you mean?" I asked. "Attack, attack from whom?"

"We don't know. Marlin brought it to me yesterday. Someone has orchestrated a calculated effort to accumulate Wade stock."

I knew who that someone was.

"In less than twenty-four hours, twenty-one percent was sold and purchased. That's a huge amount. While this could be a coincidence brought on by the cancellation of your wedding, we believe that the move was too coordinated. Marlin and I believe it has all been done by one entity. Right now, the buyer has hidden their identity under layers of shell companies."

"Was the cancellation of our wedding announced?" I hadn't heard that either.

"Julia, are you trying to keep up with the world at all?" He didn't let me answer. "The business news outlets blasted your and Skylar's picture all over their networks. As soon as they did, the perceived value of Wade began to drop. It had steadied with word of your reconciliation."

What reconciliation?

Before I could ask, Dad went on, "Then this large accumulation of stock by an unknown buyer combined with the loan issues is making the other stockholders nervous. We're back to bleeding capital and we can't hide that. The fifteen percent of stock that's currently held by single and conglomerate investors is vulnerable. If the bastard who rounded up twenty-one percent found a way to get that fifteen..."

He's not a bastard. I didn't lead with that. "If he or they did, they still wouldn't have the majority, Dad. That would only be thirty-six percent."

"Marlin is worried and so am I."

I took a deep breath. "Dad, don't trust Marlin. He was trying to get that twenty-one percent. He had a line set for sales on the thirtieth of this month. That would have taken him to forty-six percent—seven percent more than us. We would have had no choice but to go along with him on whatever deal he wanted us to take, including selling to Big Pharma. Seeing as Skylar would have voting rights to my shares after marriage, the plan was to screw us."

"How do you know this?"

"I just do, Dad." I said, retaking my seat in the comfortable chair. "Skylar didn't love me. And to be honest, I didn't love him either, not in the way you should love your husband. Our marriage was a business deal, one that had been established since we were babies in the same crib. I don't think even Skylar knew the extent to his father's conniving. Hell, he was too busy impregnating Beth."

"What did you say?" my father asked.

"I called off the wedding because I learned that my friend Beth is pregnant with Skylar's child."

"Your mother said you had cold feet."

That was what Skylar said she said.

I looked down at my feet, clad in warm socks. "My feet aren't cold, Dad. I'm not going to be Skylar's dutiful wife while he's screwing other people, and I won't be Marlin's pawn."

Dad's voice softened. "Little girl, I didn't know."

"Mom probably figured you had enough to worry about. She's asked me to come back and work everything out with Skylar."

"He doesn't deserve your effort, sweetheart. I'd give him a good piece of my mind if he hadn't left town."

"Isn't he back?" I asked.

"Back?"

"He came here yesterday," I said. "I spoke to him briefly and told him to leave."

"I don't know. I haven't seen him. As I said, some of the news and social media has the two of you off together working through your issues."

"I guarantee that we're not. I spoke to him and he left."

"Julia, I need to be honest with you," Dad said. "This could be it for Wade. And it breaks my heart. I've put my heart and soul into this company for you and your mother. I don't know if we can come back from this downturn. If this buyer isn't announced and announced as a reassurance to maintaining and helping Wade Pharmaceutical, we'll be done by the beginning of the year. We can't meet the balloon payment, and we'll have no choice but to sell."

"You don't have any clue who this buyer was?" I asked.

"Marlin had some ideas, but he couldn't prove it. He thinks it's a personal vendetta against our family. Your grandfather was selective when he chose the first investors. Some people wanted in and weren't offered that option. This could be a personal grudge that has been held since then."

Marlin was right. It was personal, but Van's grudge seemed to be more with Marlin Butler than the McGraths. I grinned, thinking about the relationship between Van and one particular McGrath, me. It was definitely friendly.

"I'm not answering my phone," I said, "but I'll watch for another secret email if you learn anything."

"I don't know how you know what you claim, but if you learn anything more, please call us."

"I will, Dad." I took a breath. "I'm sorry about the expense of the wedding."

"Compared to what we stand to lose, the wedding isn't my biggest concern. You and Wade are. Wade is our family's lifeline. I don't want it to fail."

"Me either, Dad."

"Julia, now that I know what Skylar did, I'm proud of you, sweetheart. Kick his ass to the curb."

"Thanks, Dad."

After hanging up the call, I sat for a minute in the quiet suite, trying to absorb all the information.

Why hasn't Mom told Dad where I am or about the job in Ashland?

Why hasn't she told me what is happening with Wade?

Those questions and more were going through my mind.

While Van's home was large, I was already getting

a feel for the general location of different rooms. Off the main living room toward the south wing, essentially neighboring my suite, was the library, being as the library contained both levels. My thoughts were on Wade Pharmaceutical as I mindlessly made my way back to the library and the information waiting to be deciphered.

As I descended the staircase and headed to the left, I thought about what Van had said he did.

Van said he bought and sold things.

It would make sense that he'd buy low and sell high.

If Wade's worth had dropped substantially since his accumulation of the twenty-one percent of the stock, it meant that Van bought high and the price was dropping. Van was losing money as well as my family.

Why would he want to do that?

Did he know this would happen?

I must have been lost in my thoughts and taken a wrong turn. Still on the first level in the south wing, I came to a tall set of double doors.

Is it snooping if I accidentally find it?

For a moment, I stood and listened for Margaret and Paula. I should have gone to the kitchen to see if they were done for the day. Instead, I turned the large doorknob and pushed one of the two doors inward.

My eyes widened as I took in the splendor of the room.

I hadn't found Van's bedroom suite.

I'd found his home office.

I was drawn to a table near his desk.

My stomach sank as I picked up one picture in a silver frame. I knew the man in the tuxedo. It was the woman in the white dress that I didn't know. "What the hell? You're married?"

Chapter 19

Julia

After saying goodbye to Paula and Margaret, I wandered around Van's home, searching for more mementos, something to make sense of the picture in his office. I'd been through all the possibilities in my head.

Van was married at one time.

I could live with that fact; after all, he was forty-one years old. What I couldn't fathom was why he'd kept his wedding picture up if he was divorced. And then another possibility came to me. Maybe Van was a widower. That would make sense, considering how much of a loner he claimed to be. Even Mr. Fields said Van was a private person.

The sun moved closer to the horizon and still no word from Van.

In the library, I'd begun to organize some of the things Van had accumulated. While there were flash drives with folders and folders of documents, it was the old-fashioned paper items, such as older magazines with Donovan Sherman on the cover that I perused. The headlines caught my attention.

Up and coming.

Man of the year.

Most eligible bachelor.

I checked the dates.

The most eligible bachelor magazine was from ten years ago.

If I wasn't feeling young before, I was now. Ten years ago, I was fourteen and Van was the most eligible bachelor. I flipped open the cover to the article inside. Staring down at the glossy pages, I compared the man he was then to the one I'd gotten to know now. If I were to be honest, I found him more attractive now.

There was a sense of quality to his age. It was probably that unfair issue where men aged gracefully and women just aged. However, as I looked at each picture of Van from a decade before, I believed there was a sadness existing in his green eyes that I didn't see today.

Taking that magazine to the lounge chair, I turned on a lamp and began to read. According to the article, the pictures of Van with the other women had been taken over a year before publication. Prior to the article's release date, Donovan Sherman had disappeared from the social circuit.

Each picture was captioned with Van's name, the

woman's name, the event, and date. The names of the women came from many well-known families, all with socialite names such as Nichole, Lena, Celeste, and more.

If Van was a reclusive, eligible bachelor ten years ago, when did he marry?

I went back to my laptop and pulled up his most recent biography. There was the date he was born and his parents' names.

Donovan Sherman was born in Austin, Texas, to Michael and Eleanor Thomas.

I reread the sentence.

Why isn't Donovan's last name the same as his father's or his mother's?

Another search on my computer told me that there were too many Michael Thomases and Eleanor Thomases in Austin, Texas, to even start to figure out which ones were his parents, if that was even where they still lived. For some reason, Skylar's and my wedding invitations came to mind. I remembered that more than a few of our invitations went to Texas addresses.

Closing my eyes, I contemplated going online to our wedding website. The thought of pulling the site up and seeing Skylar's and my engagement picture made the brunch Paula had prepared for me percolate in my nearly empty stomach. Another look out the window told me that night had fallen. This time of year, darkness came earlier than when the clock proclaimed it was nighttime.

The clock said only ten until six.

The one place I hadn't looked was Van's bedroom suite or up onto the third floor.

Beyond the windows the lights around the entrance to the house, garages, and driveway had turned on, shining their golden light. As I stepped from the library, I noticed the numerous lights now illuminated throughout the first floor. "Hello?" I called.

The only answer was the echo to my own voice.

No doubt there were timers or light sensors.

Crossing my arms over my chest, I took my time gazing out through the front windows. With the nightfall, I couldn't see much beyond the snowy yard. However, during the day, I'd noticed how the blanket of white appeared to be covering levels, as if his yard went down level by level until it reached the bay's shore.

Unlike the side of the house with all the lights, this side was relatively dark with only the illumination from the inside polluting the sky. Dimmed by the interior lights, I could see that the sky was peppered with stars and a low moon shone above some distant trees, giving the entire scene a blue hue.

I was about to go into the kitchen to choose which of Paula's dinners we would eat when I remembered that she said other than the holiday turkey breast, the rest were Mr. Sherman's favorites. Her eyes had glowed with excitement as she mentioned getting different ingredients for the dishes I liked.

As I turned on a few more lights, I heard the sound of doors opening.

The back entry, or entry from the garage, was similar to the front in that there were two sets of doors, one from the garage to what Margaret called the mudroom, and one from the mudroom to the house. It wasn't unusual in cooler climates for homes to be constructed that way. The middle room basically stopped the cold air from outside or the garage from rushing into the warm house.

Despite my recent findings and millions of questions, as the leaded-glass French door opened, I couldn't stop my smile. Van must have left his overcoat in the mudroom. I would be hard-pressed to answer the question of which Donovan was sexier, the GQ-suit-wearing man who was stalking toward me or the mountain man with the tight thermal shirt stretched across his wide chest.

Van didn't stop until he had me in his grasp, his

arm around my waist, pulling my hips to him. Not a word was spoken as his lips took mine.

My questions momentarily disappeared as his fingers splayed behind my head, pushing my face toward his as his lips consumed mine. All the while the fog of his expensive cologne clouded my senses. It was as his tongue joined the pursuit that I reached for his chest and my body melted against his, electrified by his touch.

My nipples beaded beneath my sweater and my core twisted.

Once our kiss separated, Van's lips turned upward as his green gaze captured mine. "I've wanted to do that since I left your suite this morning."

"I missed you."

"Is the memoir complete? Did you run out of things to do?"

I shook my head and took a step back. "The memoir is most definitely not complete. It's not started. I'm trying to figure out who you are."

Something momentarily changed in his smile. "I've told you before. Don't try. Just write what they want to read. Give them enough that the questions will be satisfied. Talk about what I did to build my businesses and my fortune."

"Is that who you are?"

He took a step forward and lifting my chin, gave me a soft kiss. "I told you, I'm the wolf."

"What happened around ten years ago?"

Van's expression became stoic, statuesque. "In my businesses? I'd need to check the timetable."

"No, with you."

He feigned a smile. "Come, Julia, can you tell me what happened to you ten years ago?"

I thought for a moment. "I can tell you exactly what happened. I was a cheerleader in the eighth grade and Bobby Gerard refused to go to the dance with me because Skylar told everyone I was taken. The same thing happened every year."

"The redundancy makes it easier to remember."

Van shrugged off his suit coat and hung it over the back of one of the breakfast-bar high stools. I watched as he loosened his dark blue tie, removed his cuff links, placing them in his pocket, and rolled up the sleeves of his blue and gray striped shirt.

There was something about a man with his sleeves rolled up that made my stomach do a flip-flop. It was probably why so many models wore their shirts that way. As Van finished the sleeves, I licked my dry lips. A smile bloomed on my face as our eyes met. "I talked to my father today."

Van went to the counter and retrieved the bottle of wine we hadn't finished last night. As he brought two glasses down from the holder over the lighted counter, he sighed. "Wade is having problems. I wasn't sure how to tell you."

"You weren't sure how to tell me that my family's entire destiny will be sold or dissolved if something doesn't happen?"

He turned, handing me one of the glasses now containing the red wine. "It's better you heard it from your father."

I swirled the red liquid around the globe of the glass. "Why is that better?"

"Because you know what can turn this all around. If I were the one who told you about the plummet of Wade Pharmaceutical's value, you'd think I planned it to get you to change your answer."

My answer to marry Van.

I hadn't thought of that. "Did you?"

"No, Julia. My plan was to stop Marlin Butler from selling Wade out from under you and your father. I didn't plan on the devaluation. In hindsight, that was wrong of me. I should have seen it coming." His green orbs came to mine. "I suppose for once I was less focused on the business futures and more on a beautiful distraction."

"Is that what I am, Mr. Sherman, a distraction?"

He nodded. "Yes. I was distracted all damn day, thinking about the way you come, the way your body trembles just before your legs stiffen. Thinking about the sweet taste of you and the mark I left on your breast."

I reached out and swatted his arm. "You did that on purpose?"

"I did."

"You're too old for things like that."

A hearty laugh filled the kitchen. "Is there anything about sex with me that makes you think I'm too old?"

"No, but...shouldn't you, I don't know, think hickeys are juvenile?"

Van set his glass on the counter and placing his hands on my waist, effortlessly lifted me to the edge of the granite. Caging me in with his arms, Van leaned forward. "No. It wasn't juvenile." His forehead came down to mine as his words slowed and his tenor deepened. "It was primitive, primal, and animalistic. It was me leaving my mark on you and telling the whole damn world that you're mine."

I lifted my lips to his for a chaste kiss. "I wasn't upset when I saw it."

"Good. Because you are mine, Julia. I found you."

My hands went to his wide shoulders. "My dad is worried, Van. Maybe if he knew it was you who bought the stock, if you told the world it was you, maybe that would stop some of the panic by the bank and other investors."

His head shook. "It wouldn't."

"Why? You have capital. You could...I don't

know...restore Wade, make the balloon payment, or give it financial backing so that it isn't vulnerable."

He took a step back and lifted his glass, bringing the rim to his lips. I watched as he swallowed and the way his Adam's apple bobbed where he'd unbuttoned his shirt. Once he was done, he began, "If the media caught wind that I was the buyer, Wade would be lucky to get pennies on the dollar in an offer from any of the bigger pharmaceutical corporations. I told you what I do."

"You buy and sell."

"I do. I also destroy."

20

Julia

My gaze narrowed. "What do you mean, you destroy?"

"I buy companies and sell them off for parts or force them to falter."

"I don't understand," I said honestly. "You would lose money."

"Sometimes and when I do, I use it to my advantage."

Four years of college courses was my big business experience. The last six months at Wade was filled with elementary tasks. With my time divided between work, wedding planning, and literature and writing interests, I didn't mind not truly being an intricate part of my family's business. I always thought I'd get the chance to do more with Wade one day. One day when I was interested.

Maybe today was that day.

"You purposely trash companies?"

"I destroy, not trash. Acquisitions are usually profitable, but when they're not, they can still be advantageous to the bottom line."

Before I asked why, the answer came to me. "When you lose money, you use it to counterbalance your gross income."

"Very good."

"What about the people who lose their jobs, careers, and livelihoods?"

"You should follow the news. Everyone is hiring."

I jumped down from the counter. "No, that's not the same thing. You're talking about taking something, a store, a warehouse, a distribution center, or a factory...a place where people have worked for generations and running it into the ground to reduce *your* tax burden."

"Not all acquisitions lose me money; however, in most cases, the acquired entity ceases to exist in its prior form." Before I could comment, he said, "Welcome to the world of big finance, Julia."

I shook my head and crossed my arms over my chest. "Oh my God, I trusted you, Van." I spun to face him. "Whether the cabin was planned or not, once you figured out who I was, you used that information to help yourself at the expense of my family's past and future."

"No. I didn't. Your family's past and future were on the chopping block before I found you or you found me."

"But you said you wanted to help."

"I still can."

I took a deep breath and slowly let it out. "You're bribing me to marry you. You're holding Wade hostage. Tell me how that makes you any better than Marlin Butler."

Van took a step toward me, a vein bulging to life in his forehead as tendons made their presence known in his neck. His tone changed. "I don't fucking have enough time to tell you all the ways I'm better than Butler." Van's voice was restrained yet forceful. "For the highlight reel, I haven't been playing your father for thirty years. I haven't been biding my time, encouraging a marriage to give me access to controlling power. And I haven't been pretending that I'm someone I'm not." He stood straighter. "This is me, Julia. You're looking at Donovan Sherman. I made myself into who I am. I don't pretend. I don't act like I'll save a failing company and then sell the business out from under them or reduce their worth to pennies on the dollar. The reason I won't tell the world that I bought that stock in Wade is because if I do, the world will believe that I bought it to make it fall. I didn't. I did it for you."

"And if I marry you, you'll save Wade."

One step and then the next, Van walked me backward until I was sandwiched between him and tall cabinets. Despite his obvious size advantage, I refused to believe no matter how worked up he'd become, that Van would hurt me. I lifted my chin, maintaining our eye contact.

His words came slower, more spaced. "I could save Wade right now, Julia. One press release announcing our engagement. No marriage yet. You said you weren't ready for that. Only an announced engagement. Giving that information to the world would be the simple gesture that would change everything. We tell the world that you, the Wade heiress, and Donovan Sherman are now engaged. We'll tell them that I have secured enough stock that together with you, we'll not only maintain but improve Wade Pharmaceutical...that statement is all it would take. I'm not bribing you. I don't pretend. I'm not a frat boy who has led you on with an agreement and fucked your best friend." He pressed himself against me. "I don't know your friend and I don't want her. I want you."

My mouth felt dry. "You've had me, Van."

"One taste of you, ten tastes, one hundred tastes...It will never be enough. That's who I am. I always want more. I won't be satisfied until we're dead."

"What?"

"Until our last breath, Julia. I can never have enough of you. I'm already addicted. I could fucking take you right now against this cabinet and again after dinner, and I'd want more."

I summoned my courage to ask one of my million questions. "Have you ever been married?" When his eyes narrowed, I added, "I would understand. Millions of people marry and divorce and find someone else. I would suspect that someone your—"

"Age," Van said, completing my sentence. "You keep bringing that up. Does my age bother you?"

I shook my head, answering him honestly. "It doesn't. I want to know you and know about you before I agree to marry."

"Agree to marry and then get to know me. Agree to marry me and tomorrow before the markets close for the holiday weekend, Wade will set records for its turnaround."

"No wedding date?" I asked.

"No date. You tell your parents you're living here, and together we tell the world we're getting married."

So many thoughts were running through my brain. "If I announce my engagement before the date of my canceled wedding, the world will blame me for what happened with Skylar. They'll think it was me who found someone else. I did, but the canceled wedding wasn't my fault."

He tilted his head as his palm came gently to my cheek. "Who gives a fuck what the world thinks?"

"I guess maybe I do."

"You shouldn't. Don't. What others think of you is irrelevant. You're strong and determined. You're smart and beautiful. Whatever misconception the world has doesn't matter. They'll judge no matter what you do. You can't win with them, don't try. Agree to the engagement and I promise Wade will turn around."

"Will you sell when it's high?"

"What happens to Wade is immaterial to me. The only thing I give a shit about regarding Wade Pharmaceutical is you. Do you want Wade to fail?"

I shook my head. "I didn't think I cared, that all I wanted was to write and explore the world...but now, hearing Dad's voice...I do care. I don't want Wade to fail. I don't want to see what my family for generations has worked to achieve be devalued and sold for nothing."

"Then...?"

I blinked as I contemplated my next sentence. There were so many unknowns about Donovan Sherman. However, I reasoned that this was only an engagement. I'd broken one of those off before. "I will agree to an engagement."

Van's lips captured mine.

When he pulled back, he grinned. "Fucking, dinner, more fucking, and then I'll call my press secretary. A statement will go out first thing in the morning before the markets open."

I smiled at Van's timeline. "I should call my parents."

He looked at the clock. "Do your parents stay up until after ten?"

"Yes."

"You can call your parents when I call my press secretary." Taking a deep breath, I nodded. "Turn around, beautiful. I'm removing those soft black pants."

My pulse quickened. "Van."

"Don't make me repeat myself."

Turning toward the cabinet, I splayed my fingers over the ivory surface as Van reached for each soft sock, removing them one by one, and then he reached for the waistband of my black pants. Soon the pants and my panties were lost to the kitchen floor. My insides twisted with anticipation as I heard the click of his belt buckle and sound of his zipper only moments before his large hands seized my hips and his foot spread my legs.

Looking down, I saw his shiny loafer and the hem of his suit pants.

I came to my toes as my back arched and my lips opened, and I let out a moan. Without foreplay or so much as a check to see if I was wet—I was—Van drove deep inside me. My body clamped down around him as my forehead fell to the cabinet.

His shoes were again in my line of vision—his

shoes and my bare feet. Van was fucking me while still mostly dressed.

In the kitchen.

The ferociousness of his initial invasion now satisfied, Van's thrusts took on a rhythm that I could anticipate. In and out. Closing my eyes, I saw us last night on the dining room table. I recalled the beauty of his cock moving in and out of me. With my hands on the cabinet, I pushed back against his thrusts, bending further at the waist, taking every inch of what he was giving me.

Despite his rule of controlling what happened during sex, I was hardly helpless in this encounter.

If I were to admit it to myself, I was also becoming addicted to this unexplainable connection we shared.

Van fisted my ponytail and pulled my head back. His warm breath came to the sensitive skin near my ear. "You're mine now, Julia. All of you." He gripped tighter, using my hair like reins as he thrust in and out. "You're perfect, perfect in every way. You feel so fucking tight. I'm the only one who ever comes in your pussy, ever."

I nodded the best I could, hearing his words while distracted by his actions.

My thoughts were consumed with the stretch and friction of his thrusts. Van filled me in a way I'd never imagined was possible.

Releasing my hair, Van's hand came to my neck, keeping my head tipped back. "Say it."

"It feels good."

He pulled my neck back farther. "You're mine. Say it. Tell me who else has ever or will ever feel how good it is to be inside you."

I struggled to breathe and yet his rhythm continued. "I'm yours, Van. Only you. Only you."

His grasp of my neck loosened, and his lips brushed my sensitive skin.

My thoughts tried to sway, to think about what others would think of our sudden engagement and to worry about all the unknowns about Van, but his attention and devotion to my satisfaction washed those thoughts away as well as anything not connected to the here and now.

Beneath my top, his large hands began to roam, tugging each breast from the lace cups of my bra, tweaking my hard nipples, and moving lower, swirling my clit. His mouth was also engaged, kissing, licking, and nipping. I was on sensory overload as my body began to tremble and we both came.

Again, my forehead fell to the cabinet as my knees weakened. After our union ended, Van spun me around and picked me up, cradling me to his wide chest. He sat me back on the kitchen counter. As his eyes met mine, he teased loose strands of my fair hair away from my face, put himself back in his boxer briefs, and secured the button on his pants.

"I can't tell you what you do to me," he said as he spread my knees and his gaze went to my core. "Fucking perfect." Before I could say a word, Van went to the sink and dampened a paper towel.

Wordlessly, I watched as he came back and gently tended to me.

The contrast in Van's unbridled passion versus this gentler caretaker was as different as night was to day. And yet as I leaned back on my arms as he prompted and he cleaned the evidence of this recent encounter, I had the revelation that Donovan Sherman wasn't one man who I could learn about in a few days. There were too many sides to him. The mysteries wouldn't go away, but with time, maybe I'd learn the secrets they kept buried.

Once Van was satisfied, he helped me off the counter and proceeded to clean the cool granite.

My large sweater hung to the middle of my thighs. After retrieving my socks, panties, and pants, I stood and my gaze met Van's. "Is there any sense in putting these back on?"

His smile warmed something within me. "That's up to you. I don't mind taking them off again."

I scanned him from his dark mane to his shiny shoes. "You're still completely dressed."

"Does that bother you?"

"I mean, I like looking at you when you're—" I was going to say naked, but honestly, Van was sexy no matter what.

"When I'm...?"

Leaving my clothes on one of the stools, I went to him, wrapping my arms around his torso and looked up. "That was hot." Warmth filled my cheeks. "I like looking at you. Period. That's the end of my sentence, Van. I find you attractive in these clothes, your mountain-man clothes, and no clothes at all."

He kissed the top of my head. "I believe dinner was next on our agenda."

I smiled. He had said 'fucking, dinner, more fucking, then calls.'

"I can warm up one of Mrs. Mayhand's dinners," I volunteered. "I was about to do that when you came home."

Van handed me my glass of wine. "Sit, beautiful. I like taking care of you."

Chapter 21

Julia

"Is everything all right?" my mother asked. "Are you on your way home? Do you need our help?"

I inhaled as I sat straighter, my phone in hand. While Van had gone to his office to call his press secretary, I'd stayed in my suite. We'd maintained the schedule Van had stated earlier in the evening—fucking, dinner, and more fucking. The second round was in my suite, in my bed. Now, after enough time to gather my breath and clean up, wearing only a robe, I stepped from the bedroom and into the sitting room with my phone in hand.

"Mom, please get Dad. I want to talk to both of you."

"Julia, tell me," she pursued, "is this something bad?"

"No." I shook my head, trying to believe my own words.

What I was about to tell them wasn't bad.

It was a shock.

"Please get Dad," I repeated.

"I'm here," he said.

"You're on speaker," Mom added.

I sat on one of the soft chairs, pulled my bare feet to the cushion and wrapped the robe around my knees. "I don't really know how to start this."

"Oh, Julia," Mom said, her voice filled with emotion. "Don't do anything rash. What Beth and Skylar did isn't your fault."

What?

"I know that, Mom."

"I've spoken to Beth. She wants to talk to you."

I rolled my eyes. I'd seen her name on my missed calls and texts. I'd deleted the texts without reading them and obviously hadn't returned her calls. "I don't want to talk to her. She can have Skylar; he's a consolation prize anyway. I hope they make each other insanely happy."

"She's hoping you two can work through this."

My head shook. "Honestly, Beth is going to be a mother. Maybe she should stop being so selfish. She got Skylar. She can't have me too."

"But, dear," Mom went on, "the two of you have been best friends since you were little girls."

"I didn't call to talk about Beth or Skylar, and I'm not coming home, not right away. I left Chicago because I wasn't ready to face everyone. Not because

I was guilty but because I didn't want to see the pity."

"You know you have a home with us," Dad said.

I had been living back in my childhood home since graduating from Northwestern. "Technically, I suppose I have a home with Skylar too. I suppose I need an attorney to look into that." I gathered my breath. "Again, none of this is why I'm calling." Before they could interrupt again, I went on. "The day I drove to Ashland, I was caught in a blizzard."

"What?" Mom gasped.

"Mom, obviously, I'm fine. But that night, I slid and ran the rental car off the road and into a snowbank. I was stuck in the middle of nowhere." I thought about that. It wasn't the middle of nowhere. It was the outskirts of where I was now.

"Julia," Dad said, "why didn't you call us?"

"Well, as luck would have it, there was no cell service. Not wanting to freeze to death in the car, I took off walking." The memories came back. "A man found me."

"Oh no."

"He was a good man. He *is*," I corrected. "He saved me. He took me to a nearby cabin and well" —I left out a few details— "neither of us knew one another. A few days later when I went to the job interview...well...it turned out that the job I came up here to explore is working for him, writing his memoir."

"Who is he?" Dad asked.

"You're working for the man who saved you?" Mom asked.

"Yes," I replied, answering my mother. "I'm working for him. Dad, he's also the buyer of the shares in Wade."

My dad's voice hardened. "Who is this man?"

"Dad, he's the reason I know about Marlin. I know that he was playing you, using me, and possibly using Skylar as a pawn to sell Wade out from under all of us. The jury is out on what Skylar knew."

"No," my mom said. "That isn't true. Whoever this man is, he's feeding you lies, Julia. Come home. Everyone who knows the truth about what happened understands why you postponed the wedding."

"I didn't postpone it." The meal we'd recently eaten churned in my stomach. "And I don't want the whole world to know."

"It's not the whole world. It's the people who matter. Even so, Skylar and Beth were wrong, but the Butlers have been our friends since before you were born. Marlin wouldn't do what you're suggesting. The person who bought the shares is responsible for the current state of Wade."

"Julia." Dad's voice was growing sterner by the

minute. "What is the name of the man who bought twenty-one percent of Wade stock?"

"His name is Donovan Sherman."

My mother's gasp was all I heard.

Does my mother know him?

Does my father?

Or do they only know Van's reputation?

"Dad, I'm telling you that despite what you may have heard about Van, he's not trying to destroy Wade. He's trying to help."

"Julia," Mom said, "I'm texting the pilot. We can get a company plane to you in a few hours." She spoke to my father. "Do you know how close we can land to Ashland?"

"Mom," I interjected, "I'm not leaving, not yet. I'm going to stay here with Van."

"That man will ruin us and ruin you," Dad said. "That's what he does."

"He won't ruin me," I replied. "I know his reputation and that's what he usually does, but this time he has an incentive to help Wade."

"What?" Dad asked. "Why would he help us?"

"Van will help because I agreed to marry him." I let out a long breath. My parents were talking, yet all I could hear was a buzz of relief. Now that I'd said the words, the tension tightening my muscles since I hit the call button began to dissipate, flowing away.

Maybe my concern was telling others, not actually being engaged again.

"Julia, this is too soon. You're on a rebound and that man is taking advantage of you."

Van had taken advantage of me but not in the way Mom meant and not in a way I minded.

"Van asked me to marry him. Together we'll have controlling interest in Wade. With Van's help Wade will thrive. He won't hurt it."

I wasn't certain if the phone on the other end had disconnected or if it was suddenly muted.

"Mom? Dad?"

It was Dad's voice I heard first. His tone was eerily calm. "You don't need to do that, sweetheart. Now that we know who bought the stock, and even without your and Skylar's marriage, Marlin and I will move forward."

"Forward? With what?"

"We came up with a plan. We can combine our stock under a legal umbrella. Together, we and the Butlers can fight whatever Sherman does. Forget about working for him or for God's sake, marrying a man you don't know—"

"I do know him, Dad. I know him, and I trust him, more than I trust Marlin. Do not combine your shares with him. Those are my shares. I don't want you to do that."

"Little girl, it's the only way to show the banks

and investors that we're strong and withstand this attempted coup."

"I'm not a little girl, Dad." I stood and paced by the fireplace and windows. "It's not a coup. Van is talking to his press secretary right now. Tomorrow before the markets open, the world will know that he bought the stock and that despite his history, he wants Wade Pharmaceutical to succeed because he's marrying me."

"Julia," Mom said, "I texted the pilot. He said we can fly directly to a small airport in Ashland. He needs to get the plane ready and file a flight plan. Once we take off, we can be there in an hour and a half."

I shook my head. "I don't want you to come here."

Mom's voice lowered. "Has he hurt you?"

He left a hickey on my left breast. I didn't say that. "No, Van hasn't hurt me. He's helped me. He's listened and now he wants to help with Wade."

"Marlin," Dad said, "will never agree to this."

"It isn't Marlin's decision."

There was a soft knock before the door to my suite opened. I spun toward him. Van's green gaze was filled with concern and inquiry, questioning my conversation. His hair was wet and his suit was replaced by a t-shirt that fit tightly over his wide shoulders and a pair of pajama pants. It was the first time I'd seen this casual attire. I lifted my hand to his chest, feeling the steadiness of his heartbeat.

"Do you want me to talk to them?" Van asked softly.

I shook my head and spoke into the phone. "Mom, Dad, I'm going to go now. Don't come here, not yet. I'm spending the holidays with my fiancé."

"Don't—"

Disconnecting the phone, I didn't hear the rest of their reply.

Van's lips curled into a grin. "I like hearing that word from you." He reached for my hand. "Are you okay? What did your parents say?"

I let out a sigh and laid my phone on a nearby table. "They were shocked." I reached for him with my other hand and looked down at where we were touching. It wasn't as dramatic as last night on the dining room table, and yet the simple comfort at having my hands in his brought a smile to my face.

Van squeezed my hands. "That's understandable."

"Dad doesn't trust that you'll help."

"He's a smart man."

My eyes opened wider. "You promised."

Van snaked his arm around my waist and pulled me flush to his chest. "He's smart because I'm the last man he or Butler should trust." His green stare met mine. "I'll prove them wrong, Julia. For you, I'll help save your family's company, but you should know that when I'm done, the Butlers will no longer be major or minor stockholders."

I stared up at him. "What's your connection with the Butlers?"

"It was a long time ago. It involved Logan first."

"Logan? You mean Uncle Logan?"

Technically, he was Skylar's uncle, but using the aunt or uncle moniker was something we did interchangeably for one another's relatives since we were young.

Van scoffed. "That's him. Marlin became involved. You can say that I hold grudges."

Chapter 22

Julia

*V*an's gaze shimmered with the gold flecks. "If you want to go home to your parents for the holidays, I wouldn't stop you. You aren't being held here against your will."

I grinned, looking down at his arm around me. "I am being held, it's not against my will, and I like it." I shrugged. "Chicago is the last place I want to be. As far as the holidays, you don't so much as have a wreath on your door. I get the feeling you're not too into celebrating."

"I've lived alone a long time. There's not a lot of festivity when you're by yourself." He took my hand and led me to the soft leather sofa. "I've already attended the obligatory parties. And I hosted the one for the Sherman and Madison executives and office staff."

"Here in your home?"

Wouldn't he want decorations if he did that?

"No," Van said, "at a restaurant in Ashland."

I leaned my head against his shoulder. "This was supposed to be a special time, a week before my wedding." I scoffed. "I had three days and two nights booked downtown at the Conrad with my bridesmaids."

"Including...?"

"I only had two, despite my mother wanting an entire court." I sighed. "If you're asking if Beth was included, the answer is yes, as my maid of honor, she was." I gave that some thought. "I suppose she wouldn't have been drinking."

"Have you spoken to Beth?"

I shook my head. "Mom said she had." My stomach twisted. "I've spoken to Vicki, the other bridesmaid. When it comes to Beth, I don't wish her ill; I just can't talk to her yet. Talking to Skylar at the hotel was enough."

Van's fingers gently ran through the length of my hair. "I've said it before, Butler's an ass."

"We had a house being built. It wasn't done." I sighed. "I imagined hosting large gatherings there."

Van reached for my chin, pulling my eyes to his. "I'm sorry."

"For what?"

"I'm sorry that you've been hurt, Julia. I'm here if you want to vent or lament. I didn't hurt you, and I never want to be someone who does, but just because you're away from your family and friends, know that I'm here. You're not alone. You never will be."

An unexpected tear rolled down my cheek.

Van wiped it away with his thumb. "Seeing you cry breaks my fucking heart. I won't lie; it also makes me want to ruin him and his entire family."

"He has a baby to support. Ruining him would hurt an innocent child."

Van turned toward the window, staring out toward the frozen bay. His jaw was set and his expression hard to read. I didn't know if he was thinking about what he could do to hurt Skylar or if his thoughts were about something else light-years away.

Before I could ask, he wrapped his arm around me.

Instead of the silence that settled around us feeling awkward, it was comforting as I laid my head back on his shoulder. The t-shirt against my cheek was soft, and his shoulder beneath was hard, the perfect pillow. "I don't need to celebrate the holidays."

It was as if my words brought Van back from his thoughts. "I have to go into the office tomorrow morning. It's Saturday and Christmas Eve. Half the exchanges will be closed before I arrive. It doesn't matter how much of a workaholic I am, I can't conduct business when everyone else around the world is unreachable." He kissed the top of my head.

"That means that I'll be back a little after noon. Unless..."

"Unless what?"

"You can come into Ashland with me. You can walk around the city, get coffee, go to the bakery, and get out of the house."

"I don't want to." I turned to him. "Margaret said I looked familiar. After I talked to my dad, I realized why. Pictures of Skylar and me have been blasted all over the business news outlets—cable networks and social media. The news of our canceled wedding was the cause of the first dip in the value of Wade. Wade's PR tried to counter it with fake news of us working out our problems."

"I saw your pictures." He grinned. "Even though I was in town, I was most certain the reports of the two of you on a Caribbean Island were exaggerated."

It was my turn to look out the window; beyond the darkness was the settled snow globe. "I'm pretty sure this isn't the Caribbean."

"And I'm not him."

"You're not." Inhaling, I let out a long sigh. "I liked Ashland when I stayed there, but I don't want to go into town and have anyone recognize me."

"Their opinions don't count."

"I'm not ready."

"You could turn in your rental car. I have more

than a few vehicles here safer than that car, ones you may drive if you want to go somewhere."

"I have a car at home." I looked up at him. "I rented one for this interview in hopes of making it more difficult to be followed." I sighed. "Have you ever felt like you don't belong anywhere, like you're lost?"

"You're not lost, Julia. You're home. If you don't want to go back to Chicago to pack your belongings, I'll have your things shipped here. You decide what will work best for you. No one else matters."

A yawn snuck up on me.

"You're tired."

I nodded.

Van stood and took my hand, helping me stand. "I have a few things I need to arrange. I can let you sleep undisturbed or..." A small smile curled his lips. "...I can come back and cuddle."

That made me smile too. "You just agreed to cuddle."

"I did."

"I am tired. There's been a lot happening." I lifted my brow as my eyes widened. "And a lot of sex."

"You can always say no."

"I don't want to say no. I feel like you've opened up a part of life that until recently I'd only heard about, a secret society where sex isn't merely an obligation but something that's enjoyed and anticipated. When Skylar and I would..." I paused and shook my head. "I'm sorry. I shouldn't talk about him so much. You don't talk about other women."

"You were engaged up until a week ago. It's been a long time since there was anyone in my life worth discussing."

The wedding picture in Van's office came back to me.

Asking him again if he was married was on the tip of my tongue.

Then again, I wasn't certain that at the moment I was prepared for the answer or the discussion that could ensue. "Skylar isn't worth discussing either," I said instead of voicing my question. "That's the point. Everything between the two of us since we were young felt like we did it because we should. You know how that first kiss is supposed to be special and make butterflies fly around your stomach?"

"Again, it's been a while. I will say I felt that and more the first time we kissed."

"The first time I've ever felt that way was with you," I admitted. "With him—kissing, petting, and later when it was more—we did it because we should. It wasn't that either of us had a burning desire."

The green in Van's eyes shimmered. "I have a burning desire."

Smiling and nodding, I replied, "So do I, Van. Red sin."

"I'll come check on you before I go to bed. If you want me to stay here, I will."

"It's your house."

"Yours too. I would like nothing more than for you to refer to here as home."

Following our kiss, Van left to do whatever he needed to do. After readying for bed, I slipped into a satin camisole and shorts and crawled into the big bed. There were a million questions and even more thoughts that should have kept me awake, but after my discussion with my parents, the only persistent feeling was exhaustion.

It took all my energy to slide under the layers of blankets. My eyes closed and the world faded away the moment I settled. At some point in the middle of the dark night, warmth radiated from another body. The room softly rattled with the sound of steady breathing.

He'd come back, not for sex but to cuddle.

Van's presence gave me more than the ability to be close. It brought to life what his earlier words had said. Being near him like this filled me with a warm glow of peace, a sense of being home, and hope that together Van and I could make it through the unknowns, finding the place where we both belonged.

Curling my body next to his, I closed my eyes and drew from his strength.

Van had the ability to buy or sell or to save or

destroy without concerns regarding the thoughts of others. While I didn't want to be unfeeling, I sought to learn from him. Opening myself up and doing as I was expected left me emotionally hurt. I didn't desire to hurt in return; I wanted to move forward. Van seemed capable of anything he set his mind to. Somewhere between falling asleep and waking, I wrapped my arm over his firm torso and vowed to learn more about this man as I learned more about me and what I was capable of becoming.

Chapter 23

Julia

*A*t nearly nine in the morning, I stood near the tall windows in the living room, gazing out over the bay, holding tightly to the warm mug filled with coffee. In Chicago we had Lake Michigan, but most of the views I'd ever seen included the tall buildings of the city. Here from Van's home I was enthralled by the natural beauty. No other structure could be seen, making the snow-blanketed view unspoiled. Wearing the camisole and shorts I'd worn to bed and the long robe, I familiarized myself more and more with Van's home. I could now make my way around the first level without taking a wrong turn.

An hour later, fresh from my shower as I opened the door to Van's office, it was on purpose.

My eyes went immediately to the table behind his desk.

The picture I'd seen yesterday was gone.

My pulse kicked up a notch as I turned all the way around, looking for the photograph somewhere else.

There were no other personal pictures to be seen in any other location. They were only located on the one table. I hadn't really looked at the other photos yesterday—I'd been too shocked by the one of Van in a tuxedo with a woman in a wedding dress. Now as I looked at each picture, I wondered if I'd imagined that one photo.

I hadn't.

I knew I hadn't.

Where did it go?

One by one, I lifted each of the other frames. There was a small aged photo, the kind that appeared to be sepia versus black and white, in a round frame. I could only surmise that these people were special to Van, perhaps his grandparents. There was another photo of a blond woman. She was pretty with striking green eyes.

Is she the woman in the other picture?

I couldn't be certain.

"Were you his wife?" I asked quietly to no one. My head tilted as I looked at her eyes. "Or are you Van's sister?"

There was another framed photo that appeared to have been taken from a distance. There were three children playing on a beach. If I were to guess, the picture had aged, but I had no other reference than that. I couldn't even make out the children well enough to assume their ages. Even the coloring of their hair was difficult to distinguish with the way the sunlight bleached the scene.

There were two other older couples. One appeared as if the photo was taken from a newspaper. "Who are these people?" I mumbled.

The last picture was of a girl. It too had been taken at a distance, but her face was visible. She was pretty with curly dark hair and a sweet smile with big front teeth.

"The information in the library wasn't enough?" Van asked, entering his office.

Jumping at the sound of his voice while feeling like a child with her hand caught in the cookie jar, I nearly knocked over the arrangement of frames. Spinning around, I stared up at Van and tried to come up with a reason why I'd be in his private office. "You said to make myself at home."

He came closer and took the framed photo of the girl from my hand. His tone and tenor were measured. "As my fiancée, there's no place in this house you aren't welcome. As the person writing my memoir, this is off-limits."

"Who is she?" I asked, tilting my head toward the framed picture now in his grasp.

Van's jaw clenched as he stared down unblinkingly at the photo.

Swallowing, I shook my head. "I'm sorry. Never mind. I overstepped."

"She's my niece." He set the picture down where it had been. "That picture was taken by a private detective that I use periodically. I'm not exactly close to my family." He feigned a smile. "Good news, my side of the wedding will be small."

"What happened with your family?" I asked, wondering if this had anything to do with his change of last name.

Van took a deep breath. "Forget about that." His smile grew and cadence changed. "I have a surprise for you."

"For me? No, not a gift. Van, I don't have anything to give—"

His finger came to my lips. "You are my gift, Julia. Don't worry about buying me anything, ever. If something catches my eye and I want it, I get it."

"It sounds like you're tough to buy for."

"I prefer the gift of watching you."

"Watching me what," I asked suggestively, thankful the conversation had veered away from my nosiness.

Van ran his finger over my cheek. "Watching your beautiful blue eyes as they swirl with emotion and passion. Your expressions speak volumes." His finger came to my lips. "When your mouth is unable to make anything but indistinguishable noises, your expression shows your every thought."

Warmth climbed up my neck to my cheeks.

"And when you blush," he said with a grin.

Pressing my lips together, I looked over at a clock. "Is it noon already?"

"No, I couldn't stay away." Van took my hand and led me out of the office, down the hallways of the south wing toward the front of the house and beyond the large living room into the foyer. We kept going through the glass doors and into the entry. Finally, Van opened the tall front door.

As the cold air swirled around us, a grin overtook my face. "You have a wreath."

Hanging from a long over-the-door hook was a giant wreath made of fresh pine and decorated with balls of gold and silver, perfect for the large door to his huge home.

Closing the door, Van led me back inside and scanned my clothes. "Go upstairs and dress in your warmest clothes. Layers are recommended."

"I've heard that."

"And your boots, coat, and I have some better gloves and a hat for you."

"Don't tell me it's the orange one."

"Orange is on purpose."

"It doesn't match my coat."

Pressing his firm lips together, Van shook his head. "Ten minutes."

"What? No. I can't be ready that fast." I started

up the stairs with the plan to thwart a rebuttal to my next sentence. "Give me half an hour."

Van looked down at his watch. "Clock is ticking."

I hurried up the staircase, excited about the unknown. I left my soft leggings on and pulled my blue jeans on over them. Two pairs of socks and a sweater over my shirt completed my layers. When I'd packed for this interview, I didn't plan on survival 101.

With five minutes to spare, I found Van in his office, behind his computer, with a cool cup of coffee. As I stepped in, my heart sank. The table behind him was completely empty. All the pictures were gone.

At the sound of my entrance, Van looked up from the screen and a smile bloomed, softening his expression. "You're beautiful."

"I look like I'm twenty pounds heavier with all these clothes."

He pushed his chair back from the desk. His earlier suit was replaced by his mountain-man clothes. As his boots clipped across the wood floor, he stalked my way and a devilish grin came to life. "I can't help that my thoughts are going to undressing you." He pulled my hips to his. "Better than unwrapping any gift you could buy."

I pulled on the collar of my second sweater. "It's getting warm in here."

"Then let's get out of here."

"Where are we going?"

"Do you trust me?" he asked.

"I do."

He reached for my hand and let out a long sigh. "I want that, Julia. I'll do my best not to spoil that trust."

I took a step back. "What's happening with Wade?"

"You haven't checked?"

"I tried. I don't have any new emails from Dad or anyone else at Wade. When I woke, I saw the article about our engagement. It was pretty basic."

"Would you rather it was detailed? I don't as a rule share private information with my PR people or the public."

I shrugged. "Honestly, it was good and to the point. I appreciated that it didn't mention my recent broken engagement."

"What you read was issued through Sherman and Madison media. The broader media has already spun it."

"Spun it how?"

He squeezed my hand. "No one else matters."

"Wade?"

"The statement has stilled the devaluation. I kept my word."

I let out a breath. "That makes me feel better."

"You can bring your phone, but where we're going there's no cell signal."

My eyes widened as excitement prickled my skin. "Are we going to the cabin?"

He tugged on my hand. "Come with me."

Soon we were both in his big black truck and heading back down his long lane. Beyond the windows, the sun glistened on the fallen snow. The heater filled the cab with warm air as Van took some barely marked narrow roads. All at once, the cabin came into view. "Is it silly that I'm excited about a one-room cabin?"

He parked the truck. "No. I am too. This cabin holds some wonderful memories." He grinned. "Recent memories."

I returned his grin, the same recent memories flooding my mind.

Van reached for my hand. "Well, first I'll get the fire going and then the real work begins."

"Work?"

Van's green stare went out the windshield to the forest surrounding the cabin. "Yes, we have a tree to find."

"A tree?"

We both walked to the cabin on a newly shoveled path. When he opened the door, on the floor near the small kitchen area were bags and boxes. "Van?"

"It's not easy to find decorations on Christmas Eve. I may have pillaged these decorations from my office. By the time we're done, the cabin will be festive and ready to celebrate."

Van's desire to celebrate for me, something he claimed he hadn't done as of late, brought the holiday to life in a way that decorations alone could never do.

I looked from Van to the window. "I've never cut down my own tree."

Van reached for my hand and brought it to his lips. "Another first."

As Van started the fire in the stone fireplace, I straightened the bed as it was as we'd left it. I also found some food Van had already delivered to the cabin and organized it along the small counter. The jug of water made me laugh. "No boiling water."

"There are advantages to being prepared."

The flames snapped and crackled as the kindling caught fire. Soon the chill within the small cabin began to fade.

"Are you ready to find the perfect tree?" Van asked, his green orbs shimmering in the firelight.

I pulled the orange hat down over my hair and ears. Apparently, the color orange signaled to hunters that we were people not animals. No one should be hunting on Van's property, but it was better to be safe. I pushed my hands into the wool-lined mittens. "I'm ready."

Chapter 24

Julia

With an ax in his other hand, after closing the cabin door, Van took my hand, our mittens wrapping around one another's grip. My total experience around the area of the cabin was limited to the journey to and from the truck and to and from the outhouse. This time, we headed into the forest, our boots sinking in the deep snow.

"They're all so tall," I said, looking up through the big trees to the blue sky above. I wasn't only speaking of the pine trees, but also deciduous trees such as the white birch whose white trunks highlighted the landscape.

"There are places on my land where I've planted saplings," Van said. "I'm hoping at least one will still be small enough."

"You planted trees? There weren't enough?"

Van grinned, looking down at me with pink cheeks from the cold. "There's never enough."

"Oh," I said with a shake of my head. "I forgot."

"When I decided to live here, I purchased multiple five- and ten-acre lots. Many had structures. Some were willing to sell, others needed convincing. I had most of the structures demolished. Those spaces then needed trees."

"How did you convince people to leave their homes?"

"Everything has a price."

I gave that some thought as we trudged forward. "You didn't want any other buildings?"

"I kept a few, but nothing I chose to keep is too close to the house."

Taking a deep breath of cool air, I stilled. "You know, I think I'm in pretty good shape."

"I think you're in fantastic shape."

"Then why is walking through this snow wearing me out?"

Van laughed. "Just wait until we have to drag the tree."

"I think we should have considered cross-country skis."

"We should have. A snowmobile would have been a good idea too." He grinned as his words came out in vapor puffs. "Next time."

Those words were so simple and yet held more meaning than I could comprehend.

Next time inferred there would be more times like

this, more times with the two of us and adventure. It was unfamiliar to me to imagine spending so much time alone, only the two of us. Skylar was all about appearances. Together meant out to eat at one of Chicago's finer restaurants, the symphony, or the philharmonic, where we were going the night I walked out on him.

Van's and my journey continued for another fifteen to twenty minutes, at times walking through knee- and thigh-high accumulations of snow. The good news was that due to the excessive cold temperatures, the snow was basically powder and easier to be displaced than heavier snow farther south. Cresting a hill, I saw what Van had described. The giant pine trees were gone, replaced by smaller ones.

At first, I was preoccupied with walking between the trees, comparing their height to Van's and mine. Even the smaller ones seemed too big when I thought about putting it in the one-room cabin. When I looked up, the cold air caught in my lungs.

The scene before me was simply spectacular—the crystal-clear sky above and the beautiful white bowl.

"This view is gorgeous," I said, my words floating through the air in puffs of vapors. "I bet it's amazing in the summer."

Van pulled me close, looking down at me. "My view is stunning, no matter the season."

"Honestly, Van, how did you choose which home

to keep? If they all had beautiful views like your house, it must have been difficult."

"Location. I wanted to be remote. Where we are is a lot closer to the edge of the property and to the civilization of Ashland. Some of the homes were older. I weighed the pros and cons. The one where we live won. I had it gutted. The contractor said it had the best bones, making it sturdy. It was also near the size I wanted." He grinned. "With room for expansion. More. Bigger. Better."

I spun toward the younger trees. "I feel bad that you're going to chop down one of these. They're just babies."

"There are hundreds if not thousands on the property." He lifted my chin with his gloved hand. "You have a beautiful heart, Julia. I tell you what, we chop down one for our celebration and in the spring, we plant ten or one hundred more."

"We can do that?"

"We can do whatever we want."

After we decided on one of the smaller pines, I stood back as Van knelt in the snow and began chopping the tree. First, he chopped off the lower branches before his ax began notching the trunk.

As the ax flew with vigor and force, I wrestled with the dichotomy of the man Donovan Sherman. The man my parents warned me about was such a small part of him. I truly didn't know all there was to know about him, but I was getting to know the man that others didn't.

A smile came to my cool lips as I remembered the way Van warmed our dinner and cleaned the plates after we ate, and the way he fed me with coffee and nectarines. This man working up a sweat in the cold air was the one who chopped wood for a fireplace that saved me from freezing.

Would the people who only know Van as a business tycoon recognize the man before me?

"Timber," Van called as the pine fell to the soft snow.

He handed me the ax. The pass-off made me wobble as I tightened my grip. "That's a lot heavier than I thought."

I wasn't good at judging weight, but now that I held the handle of the ax, I was even more impressed with the way only a few minutes earlier, Van had been rapidly reeling it at the tree's trunk.

"Here's the hard-work part."

Van held tight to one of the bottom branches as he began to drag the tree, backtracking our journey back to the cabin. Our speed was slower as we continued toward the cabin. As we neared, the thin plume of smoke could be seen coming from the chimney. By the time we made it back, the sky was beginning to lose its sunlight, with shadows appearing on the eastern horizon.

The heat from the fire within the cabin hit like a wall as we entered. The layers that were so essential outside were now stifling. Sighing, I removed the mittens and ugly orange hat, hanging them from the pegs near the door. It didn't take a mirror to know my hair was a mess. Pulling the tie from the end, I ran my fingers through the length and piled it all high on my head.

If it was going to be messy, why not be a messy bun?

As I began to lessen the cumbersome layers, Van dragged the tree to the hearth. He said it was only for a little while to melt the snow.

With the addition of a few more logs, the fire roared, its flames crackling within the sandstone hearth.

Soon, Van's coat, hat, and gloves were also hanging on the pegs near the door. And both sets of our boots were there. As I continued losing the layers, I watched Van. His meticulous movements, his knowledge of what it took to stay alive and warm in this remote cabin, and his strength with the ax and tree had me enthralled. When his gaze caught mine, I smiled. "Thank you."

"Was this your first hike through drifted snow?" he asked, his green orbs reflecting the fire's flames. "I'm working for more firsts."

I shook my head. "More?"

"Always more, Julia."

I went to him, grinning at his messy dark hair and laid my palm on his chest, feeling the warm thermal shirt and his beating heart. "Yes, it was my first hike through the snow to find the perfect tree. My trees have always been artificial."

Van exaggerated a gasp.

I grinned. "You didn't even have a tree."

"But artificial?"

"I had one of those tall thin ones in my apartment during college, but the ones at my parents' home just appeared one day fully decorated and then after the New Year they went away. I guess you could say, I'm not very experienced in decorating trees myself."

"You're creative. I'm sure together we can figure this out."

"Does that mean that you're not experienced either?"

"It means that I've never thought about it. I suppose as a child I helped decorate the family tree, but if memory serves me, I avoided those bonding moments. And as you saw at the house, decorating hasn't been a priority." He reached for my cheeks. "Priorities can change."

His lips met mine.

Thinking about our hike, I added, "I've been cross-country and downhill skiing, but hiking through those drifts was definitely a first." I smiled. "The thank-you I said earlier was for something else."

Van's hands came to my waist, his warming fingers splaying beneath my sweater. "What are you thanking me for?"

"For showing me a side of Donovan Sherman that the world doesn't see."

His grasp of my torso tightened. "Julia, this is a Donovan Sherman I haven't seen in a long time—I'm not sure if I ever have. This is what you do to me; you make me want to be better and to make you happy."

"You make me happy. You don't need to try."

"I do. My first instinct is to be selfish." He reached for the hem of the sweater and pulled it over my head. Despite the fire's warmth, my nipples beaded. Van took a deep breath. His gaze focused on my silk camisole covering my lace bra. "You're so beautiful."

I lifted his chin, already prickly from his morning shave. When his green gaze met mine, I smiled. "I'm happy. I'm unbelievably happy. You do the same thing to me, Van. You make me feel like a different person. When I'm with you, I feel liberated."

Every word was true.

Under his wanton gaze, I felt a sense of sexual power and prowess I'd never before felt. His obvious desire filled me with strength to be more assertive than I'd ever been. I pushed up on my tiptoes and pressed my lips against his.

My hands went to his belt as I fell to my knees.

"Julia." His voice was suddenly an octave lower than it had been moments ago.

Peering up through my eyelashes, I smiled as my fingers worked to release his belt buckle, the button and zipper of his jeans. "It's my turn, Van. I want to give you something to show you how much I appreciate all you've done for me."

"Fuck." The one word was drawn out.

As I freed his hardening cock from his boxer shorts, I licked my lips. Lapping the pre-come from the glistening tip, I opened my lips as my hands worked the root and gently squeezed his balls. Inch by inch, I took him, each time backing away, each time taking more.

With his tip teasing the back of my throat, I sealed my lips and ran them and my tongue up and down. In the short time since I'd fallen to my knees, his cock had gone from hardening to rock solid. When I looked up, I saw the combination of restraint and pleasure in his expression. Van's chin was lifted and the muscles and tendons of his neck stretched. His arms and hands were at his side, the tension visible with his fisted fingers.

This wasn't my first blow job, but it was the first one I wanted to do because of the desire bubbling within me and the first one I wanted to be sure I did right.

The sound of a pop echoed through the cabin as my lips came off his steel-hard rod. I reached for Van's hands. When his eyes met mine, I placed his hands on top of my head, over my messy bun. "Use me, Van. I want to do this right."

His fingers splayed over my head, before dropping to my cheeks. "If you don't think what you're doing is right, you're not paying attention."

His erect penis bobbed before me.

I grinned. "I'm paying attention. I've invited, now I want you to lead."

"Fuck, Julia. I don't want to hurt you."

My tongue licked his length from the tip until his coarse hair tickled my face. "You won't. Use me."

Van's chest inflated and deflated with each deep breath. His hands came back to my hair. "You're doing well. Open your lips, Julia."

I did as he instructed.

"Rest your tongue and close your lips. I'm going to fuck your mouth."

I nodded.

His cock slid within my mouth as I closed my lips. My eyes closed as Van began to move, pushing deeper each time. I concentrated on not gagging as my core became wetter and wetter with his wordless noises of pleasure. My hands went to his strong thighs as Van continued pistoning his hips. It was as his grip tightened and his speed increased that I knew he was close.

When he tried to pull away, I wrapped my arms around his legs, refusing to not follow through on what I'd started.

"Fuck, Julia, I'm going to come."

I held tighter to his legs as his cock began to throb, my mouth filled, and I rapidly swallowed. The cabin filled with Van's mumbled curses as I stayed on my knees, licking and sucking until he was satisfied and clean. When I looked up, I saw a gaze filled with so much emotion that I would fall to my knees every damn day to see it again.

"You're..." He didn't finish his sentence. He offered me his hand.

"I'm?" I asked as I stood and leaned into him.

"More. Every second of every day, you're more."

"That's what you want, isn't it?"

"More than I knew."

I looked around. The sky beyond the windows was dark. "I know I just had a protein snack..." —my cheeks warmed— "but I could make us some food while you get our tree in its stand and then we can decorate it."

Chapter 25

Julia

*V*an wrapped his arm around me as we both stared at the tree. He'd taken strands of garland of silver and gold, silver beads, and white, gold, and silver ornaments from his office. I imagined one of his employees showing up and wondering who vandalized the tree. My guess would be that the CEO would be their last suspect. He had left the lights. Without electricity, they wouldn't do us much good.

"It's the best tree I've ever seen," I said, leaning against his side.

His head tilted the same direction as the slightly leaning tree. "It's definitely interesting."

I pushed up on my tiptoes and kissed his cheek. "It's hard to believe we were here only a week ago."

Taking my hands, Van's gaze washed over me. "Finding you was the best thing I've done in my whole life."

A smile lifted my cheeks. "That's a long time."

His head shook. "It's enough time to make a lot of mistakes. This—between us—has been a whirlwind, but it's not a mistake."

"I agree. A mistake wouldn't feel this good."

Our dinner was behind us and our stomachs filled as we sat cross-legged together on the pile of rugs before the fireplace. It was the exact same place we'd had those nectarines and mugs of coffee a week earlier. The flames flickered and snapped as the damp wood hissed and spit.

The silence settled around us, cocooning us in our cabin in the snow globe, when finally, Van spoke, "My niece is ten years old. Her name is Brooklyn."

I turned, watching Van's profile. What he was saying was a gift to me, even more so than our festive decorations. His protruding brow furrowed and his jaw clenched as he stared at the flames. I started to ask if she was his sister's child, since Margaret had asked if I was Van's sister, but before I spoke, he went on.

"She's my brother's daughter. He and I haven't spoken for over a decade."

I laid my hand on his jean-clad thigh, silently encouraging Van to continue.

He let out a long breath. "He and his wife were having some financial problems. I'd already walked away from my family and had achieved what many would consider success." His nostrils flared. "I fucked up. If I were him, I wouldn't talk to me either."

"What happened?"

"I wanted more. Nothing was ever enough. I wanted every asshole who ever stood in my way or ever doubted me to suffer."

As his confessions wafted through the air, I chanced another question. "Did you want your family to suffer?"

He nodded.

"Your brother?" It could be why he wasn't welcome to see Brooklyn in person.

"Yes."

I waited.

"I succeeded." Van stood and went to the kitchen area, filling two mugs with coffee. When he came back and handed me one, he feigned a grin. "Maybe I should have brought something stronger?"

Bringing the rim of the mug to my lips, the strong aroma of coffee overtook the lingering pine scent. "I think this is plenty strong." I patted the spot where he'd been sitting. "You don't need to tell me more if you don't want to. I promise that none of this will be in your memoir."

His green orbs snapped to mine. "I'm telling you this because you agreed to marry me, Julia. It has nothing to do with the memoir. Like I've said, I want the memoir for one reason." He shrugged. "Maybe two. First, I am sick and tired of the rumors and untruths that resurface on and off about how I made my money."

"And the second?"

"It goes back to what I said, wanting every asshole who stood in my way or doubted me to see in print that despite them, I have succeeded."

I smiled at his claim of success in the past tense. I'd bring it to his attention, but I didn't want him to change his mind. "Maybe it wasn't despite those people but because of?"

Van placed his mug on the hearth and then leaned back on his outstretched arms. "No."

"No?"

"No, those people don't deserve an ounce of credit."

"I'm getting the theme of your memoir. Were there any people along the way who deserve credit?"

He hesitated. "Yes. A handful."

"Are you willing to acknowledge them in print?"

"Some of them, yes. I didn't start out knowing everything. I still don't. My need to achieve narrowed my focus. I've been fortunate enough to run into people who took the time to teach me," he scoffed, "after kicking my ass."

"What?" I asked with a giggle. "You're admitting to having your ass kicked?"

"Those people would never have gotten my attention without first proving that they knew more than I did. There was one in particular." Van shook his head. "I never imagined talking about this. I figured, give the information, read the draft, dictate changes..."

"If it makes it easier, as you know, I've never interviewed anyone for information on a memoir."

His hand landed on mine. "I'm getting off on all these firsts."

The pink of my cheeks from our earlier hike and the firelight increased. "I can help with that."

He squeezed my hand. "Oh, you already did."

"Who was the one in particular?" I asked.

"The one who comes to mind is Lennox Demetri."

I shook my head. "I don't recognize the name."

"Those people involved in finance who read the memoir will."

"Has he been in high finance" —the term Van had used— "for a long time?"

"Yes, and he's only a few years older than me." Van inhaled. "I think it's why I respect him so much. Despite what you think of my age, Lennox isn't old. He had an advantage I didn't. He had the advantage of a father who led the way."

"Had? Is his father deceased?"

"I meant *had* as in Lennox had a road map that I didn't have."

"Was your father" —I thought about the name difference— "interested in high finance?"

"My parents are irrelevant. They fucked and gave birth to a son. That was their contribution. They don't need to be mentioned. I'd prefer they weren't. One of my first muses taught me that life didn't have to be stagnant. Wipe the dust of the past off your shoes and never look back."

I gathered my strength and forged ahead. "Why is your last name different?"

Van's lips formed a straight line as he turned toward me. "Was that in the information I gave you to use?"

"No, it was in an online biography I read the other day."

"One of my first significant acquisitions was a well-known regional chain of department stores. There are many reasons why it was floundering, not limited to the mismanagement from the top. It had been around for generations and was existing on its name alone. This was over fifteen years ago. People considered me too young to accomplish what I had. I'd made money, but not—"

"Enough," I interjected.

Van nodded. "I realized I needed to do more than acquire. With changes in tax law, I understood that liquidation would do more for me than make a business profitable. I set my sight on that chain."

"Was there a reason?"

"Both of my parents had been employed by the chain for their entire lives. My mother started as a cashier and worked her way up to buyer. She would fly to New York and Europe for fashion shows and help decide what fashions the stores would sell. My father began in accounting at a regional store and moved up to corporate."

"You targeted an entire chain of stores to hurt your parents?" My stomach twisted.

"I did, Julia. I won't lie to you and pretend I'm a good man. I'm telling you the truth. I purposely worked to acquire the entire chain and purchase the name that was recognized throughout multiple states. Buying the name was crucial because if I hadn't, theoretically, senior members of the founding family could restart a new chain with the old name. The average shopper wouldn't recognize that it was different."

"What happened?"

"I succeeded. In the process, I liquidated everything and walked away with a substantial profit. During the process, I was blamed for things that were not my doing. I didn't care. Their mistakes added to my reputation."

"Like what?" I asked, wondering what would be horrible enough for family members to turn their backs on one another.

"I told you that my people watch for vulnerability. It was a lesson I learned well with this first major acquisition. The chain was having financial problems, spending multiple years in arrears, drowning in debt. One of their last-ditch efforts was to access the employees' retirement pensions."

I gasped. "No."

Van nodded. "The original owners were able to deplete the accounts through a loophole. Of course, their plan was to make money and repay the funds before the employees learned the truth. It didn't happen that way. The employees learned that their retirement funds were gone when they also learned their jobs were terminated."

"Could you have helped them?"

Van shrugged. "I didn't want to, Julia. I wanted them to suffer."

"Why?"

"My parents know why."

"Do you regret it?" I asked.

"No. That deal propelled me higher than I thought was possible. Compared to where I am now, it was minimal. However, without that acquisition, I wouldn't be Donovan Sherman."

"And why is your name different?"

"Because in the early negotiations of that particular deal, I petitioned for a name change."

I tried to think of department stores that had

gone away during my lifetime. There were more than I could recall. "Why Sherman?"

"Because once that deal was complete, Sherman Brothers department stores ceased to exist."

"And Donovan Sherman was born," I said, with an odd, eerie feeling.

"Yes."

"Why?"

"Because even though I don't talk to my family, my name is a reminder of what I did to them." He sighed. "It also reminds me of what I've done and what I'm capable of doing."

"It wasn't only them," I said, thinking of the other employees.

Van shrugged.

"Did you just tell that story to the writer of your memoir?"

"It's a matter of public record that Donovan Sherman first came on the scene roughly fifteen years ago. It's also public record that I changed my name from Thomas to Sherman." He looked from the fire to me. "You found that online."

"I found your parents' names. I didn't search to find why theirs were different than yours. I guess maybe I wanted to learn it from you."

"Who I was before that name change wouldn't be Donovan Sherman's story."

There were so many questions I had, and yet, as I

stared at Van in the firelight, I mostly wanted to comfort him. I leaned closer and offered a soft kiss on his prickly cheek. A quick glance at my watch told me that the clock had struck midnight. "Merry Christmas, Van."

"What do you want, Julia? If I could give you anything, what would that be?"

I looked around the one-room cabin, feeling the warmth of the fire, inhaling the aroma of pine, and seeing the decorated tree. My attention went back to the man beside me. "I can't think of anything I need."

"Need and want are two different things." He ran his finger down my cheek, stopping at the edge of the camisole, pushing it downward between my breasts. His smile grew as he looked back up at me. "A week and a day ago, if I'd been asked what I needed, I would have said nothing. My needs have been met since I completed that deal. I've spent the years since concentrating on what I want. More land, more money, and more power. I didn't need a thing. That changed. It changed in this cabin."

I sucked in a breath as his deep tenor reverberated through me.

"I want you," he said. "I want you over and over, but it's more than that. You changed everything. Now I need."

"What do you need?"

"I need to know you're happy, safe, and protected.

I need to have you at my side. I need to fall asleep beside you and wake in the same place. Will you let me do that for you?"

The scene blurred with tears I didn't expect. "That sounds like a proposal. I already said I'd marry you."

"I didn't propose before. You deserve that."

I wrapped my arms around his neck and lay myself against his wide chest as his arms came around me. With my forehead on Van's shoulder, I nodded. Just the two of us alone before the fire felt right, much righter than in front of a room full of people. I lifted my head and looked into his gaze. "I didn't know I needed that, to hear you ask, but I did."

Van gently lay me back on the rugs and followed me until he was over me, our noses touching. "Will you, Julia McGrath, be my wife?"

My eyes opened wide as the picture of him with a woman in wedding attire came to mind. "You said you've never proposed before?"

"Only to you. I think, unofficially, this is the third time."

What does that mean about the picture he had in his office?

I didn't want to ask, not now.

"My answer is yes. I promise it won't change."

Chapter 26

Van

Even though I'd gotten up twice throughout the night to add wood to the fire, I woke to the chill of the air upon my face. Julia's soft curves and flat planes brought more than warmth to my body beneath the blankets.

As I reached for her, I had a moment of concern, worried that Julia was sore and worn out from my insatiable desires. Perhaps they weren't insatiable, but they'd been backed up by years of denial. Finding her was the final crack in the dam of restraint. Now the flood was out of control.

With her round ass beside me, I turned, spooning her warm body. Her long blond hair tickled my nose and my cock was coming to life. Despite her soft, measured breathing, my hands roamed, caressing and stroking until her long lashes fluttered and she whispered my name in that sleepy, just-awakened voice.

"I've got you," I whispered against her ear as she wiggled, pushing herself back as I pushed forward.

My eyes rolled with pleasure as together, with my pushing forward and her pressing backward, my dick became sheathed by her perfect pussy.

"Tell me no," I prompted.

Julia shook her head. "Don't stop, Van."

Wrapping my arms around her, I moved slower than last night in front of the fire and again in the bed. With Julia in my arms, surrounded by the cool morning air, for once that I could recall, I wasn't in a hurry. The urgency from before dissipated like the vapors from our words as we found pleasure in one another in what Julia called our snow globe.

With one of her breasts in each of my hands, I tweaked her nipples as I continued moving in and out. She leaned forward and pressed her hips back, taking me deeper than before. Her fingers gripped the sheet as I took her, slow and steady.

"Oh God, Van. Faster."

A smile came to me as I slowed, purposely teasing her.

Her legs wiggled as she pushed toward me. Each time she did, I backed away, keeping us connected, barely. I pulled out and rolled her toward me. Julia's blue eyes swirled as they met mine. "Are you trying to tease me by not letting me come?"

"I am."

Her lower lip came forward in the cutest pout as her gaze turned sultry. I took a deep breath as her fingers wrapped around my cock, moving up and down. I tugged her hand away. "Oh, beautiful, my coming isn't in question."

I leaned back on my heels with my erect cock bobbing between us. "Merry Christmas," I said with a grin. "I know what I want."

"What do you want?"

"I want to watch you come." I pushed her ankles back, exposing her core. "Show me how you masturbate."

Her eyelids grew heavy and her breaths came quicker as she contemplated my request.

I reached for her hand and led it to her core. "Do I need to repeat my gift request?"

"What if I told you that I don't?"

"That you don't masturbate?" I scoffed. "I wouldn't believe you. Up until recently" —I lifted my eyebrows— "very recently, you've had an extremely unsatisfying sex life."

She took a deep breath before her fingers found her clit, rubbing circles, slow at first. Julia was stunning as her blue orbs lost focus. Her fingers moved faster as her breaths came quicker. Faster still, her legs stiffened. It was as she tightened her torso, pushing her pelvis upward that I seized her hand, stopping her display.

Her eyes opened wider. "Hey. You're a sadist."

"No, I'm not. I have it from here."

I encouraged her to move onto her hands and knees. With her perfect ass in the air, I stopped teasing and plunged deep inside. Julia screamed out burying her face into the pillow as all at once she imploded, her body strangling my cock as her arms and legs trembled.

Making her wait had the result I wanted. The orgasm that overtook her came fast, but it wasn't short-lived. Julia was still shaking as I plunged in and out, finding my own release. Slowly, I separated our connection, lying beside her and pulling her to me until we were nose to nose.

Just catching her breath, Julia filled the cabin with giggles and sighs as she lifted her arms around my neck. "That was so mean," she finally said, a huge smile overtaking her face.

"I'll never do it again."

Her head shook. "Oh my God, if you don't, I'm divorcing you. I've never come that hard."

"Good news, your unsatisfying sex life is over."

"That is good news," she said, dropping her face on my bare chest.

"I should go feed the fire," I said.

"Don't leave me." Her eyes opened as she lifted her chin to make eye contact. "What is on our agenda?"

"Spend the entire day like this."

"I like that. I'd love to do another hike. It was

cold and hard to walk in the snow and at the same time, I loved every minute of it."

"There's plenty of untouched land around the house, and I have an easier way to travel."

"We're going back to the house?" She pouted. "The house has internet and cell service. I like the un-connect-ability of our snow globe."

"The house also has showers," I offered.

"Good point, but is it bad that I want to stay hidden here with you through today?" She leaned back and looked at me closer. "Do you need to get back for work?"

"Do I need...? My only needs are to make you happy. If hiking here will make you happy, then that's what we'll do. Back in the garage, I have snowmobiles. We can explore my land and out on the bay. There are trails everywhere."

Her eyes opened wide. "On the bay? Is it safe?"

"We should probably wait a week or two, but the ice here gets thick enough to drive from the mainland to Madeline Island up near the Apostle Islands."

She shook her head and smiled. "What if I told you I've never ridden on a snowmobile?"

A smile curled my lips. "Maybe we should construct a list of all these firsts...first time to have sex, first time to have an off-the-chart orgasm, first time cutting down of a Christmas tree—"

Her small finger came to my lips. "Hearing you

say all of those firsts makes me think I've never really lived."

"Oh, you've lived, beautiful. Now you're alive."

As she curled against me and my arms surrounded her, I questioned my presence.

Is Julia McGrath truly a gift I don't deserve?

Was she lost on a snow-covered road on the outskirts of my property to save me from myself and my lonely exile?

Will she save me?

Is it fair to ask her to do that?

I ran my hand over her loose long hair, smoothing it away from her beautiful face.

Has my penitence been paid?

Do I deserve to move forward, or will I bring Julia down and ruin her like I do anyone else who makes the mistake of trusting me?

Wade Pharmaceutical came to mind.

I'd told the truth; the perceived value of Wade Pharmaceutical had stabilized. It would take a good-faith measure on my part to not only stop the bleeding that Julia's broken engagement had started and my purchase of stock had exacerbated but increase the value. If I didn't make that move this next week, it could be too late.

Later in the morning, I stood in my boots, jeans, and coat, waiting in the cold morning air. With her nude body wrapped in a blanket and wearing her snow boots, Julia stepped out of the outhouse and grinned. She had her long hair piled on top of her head in a large bun as she'd done last night after our hike.

"That warm shower might not be a bad idea," she said with a grin.

The sky above us was beginning to fill with light. Unlike the clear day we'd had yesterday, growing gray clouds shone pink on the eastern horizon.

"What are you thinking?" she asked as I stared out at the pink morning.

"More snow is coming. We have enough food to stay here. After all, there's no decoration at the house."

"There's a wreath." She leaned toward me. "I'll be snowed in with you wherever you want." Her eyes opened wider. "Mrs. Mayhand prepared us a holiday dinner with a turkey breast and delicious sides."

The food I'd brought paled in comparison. "Once we're home, if you want to go for a hike or ride, I volunteer to be your tour guide."

She bounced on the toes of her boots as we went back to the cabin. "I accept and I want to ride the snowmobile. Can I drive?"

I shook my head. "That's a first that can wait."

After dressing, eating the muffins I'd bought at my favorite bakery in Bayfield, and drinking some fresh coffee, Julia and I took the time to strip the bed and make it with fresh sheets. She took the dirty ones out to the truck. We'd wash them at home, and I'd bring them back here. We collected all of our food. The reason I kept soup out here was because in the cans it didn't attract animals or bugs.

There weren't bugs in the winter, but there were animals. Black bears weren't as common as they used to be in these parts and currently, they'd be hibernating. Nevertheless, I didn't want any other mammal to smell food and make himself at home.

After I poured water over the remaining hot coals, I took Julia's hand before going out to the truck. The tree was still standing in the corner covered in decorations.

"Should we undecorate and take it outside?" she asked.

Common sense told me that we should. The small fraction of a romantic in me considered coming back for the New Year. Maybe by then I'd have a ring to present to my fiancée. I took a deep breath. "I say we leave it for now."

Julia nodded. "We can come back here anytime. This place holds wonderful memories."

It was completely new for me to think of memories with a smile.

New memories...those were what I wanted with Julia.

As we drove away from the cabin, and toward the house, my mind was filled with places where I could lead Julia on my land and on the trails beyond. Each vista and outlook came to my thoughts, wanting the perfect place for the perfect woman.

With my mind in an unusually positive place, I didn't notice the tire tracks until we came to the driveway before the house. I stopped the truck before driving onto the cement.

Fuck. I should have closed the gate near the main road. "Someone has been here."

Julia sat forward. "Mrs. Mayhand?"

"She wouldn't come on Christmas."

Julia's gaze widened. "Her son-in-law?"

"I'll park the truck. Before we go inside, let me check the security." I pushed the button, opening one of the garage doors.

"Could whoever it is be inside?" Julia asked.

"No. No one could get inside without tripping the security," I said, hoping I was right. My pulse sped up as I pulled my phone from the cupholder. I'd turned it off to save the battery, since I'd left it in the truck. I hit the power button.

The screen came to life.

I hit the security icon and let out a breath. "No one is inside."

"What if it was my parents?"

"If it was, they found us gone."

Julia's smile dimmed. "I don't want to go back with them."

"You're an adult. You don't have to go anyplace you don't want to."

She reached for my hand. "I see that now...you helped me see it."

"Let's go." While I was confident that the house was safe, I wasn't sure who had been here, making their way onto my private property all the way to my home.

My phone vibrated in my hand with numerous notifications—text messages and emails. I shook my head. Most were from my legal team and a few missed calls from Connie, my assistant, beginning yesterday afternoon.

Whatever the fuck was going down was looking for me.

I needed to face it.

Donovan Sherman didn't hide or back away.

Once we were inside and had our coats hung in the front closet, I laid a kiss on Julia's head. "I have messages to return."

Her eyes narrowed. "My phone is upstairs. If your messages are about Wade or my family, will you tell me?"

"I'll never lie."

Julia nodded. "I'll go shower and change clothes."

My eyes stayed fixed on her as she walked away, up the staircase and toward the south wing.

There was more to what I'd said. I wouldn't lie; however, some things will never be said.

I headed toward my office as I hit the button to call Connie. She answered right away.

"This is Christmas," I said. "You're supposed to be celebrating."

"Mr. Sherman" —her concern filled tone held my attention— "it's about Phillip." When I failed to reply, she clarified, "Phillip Thomas."

I closed the door to my office as heat began to build beneath the layers of my clothing. Gritting my teeth, I asked, "What about him?"

"He saw the announcement of your impending engagement."

Running my free hand over my hair, I gripped the phone tighter. "I don't care what my brother reads—"

"I didn't want to bother you with this...yesterday or today...but he was upset, demanding to speak to you. He sounded...off. I explained that you were unreachable."

"We haven't spoken in a decade."

"He said if he isn't able to speak to you about his issue with you marrying, he'll speak to your new fiancée."

Over my dead body.

"Did you give him either of our private numbers?" I asked.

"No. I wouldn't do that. I wanted you to know what he said."

Now I knew.

Despite the irritation Connie's information rekindled, the saying *don't shoot the messenger* came to mind. Taking a deep breath, I replied, "Thank you, Connie. Let me know if he calls again."

"I will. And sir, Mr. Fields has been trying to reach you."

"Thank you. I'll call him next. And..." —there was no doubt that Julia's goodness was affecting me— "have a good holiday."

"Thank you," she said with the sound of relief. "You too, Mr. Sherman."

As I disconnected the call, I realigned my thoughts. If a confrontation with Phillip occurred, it wouldn't end over *my* dead body.

It would end over his.

Chapter 27

Julia

Turning on my phone, I kicked off my boots, wiggling my sock-covered toes in the soft, warm rug near my bed. Much as Van's phone had done, my phone vibrated and dinged with numerous incoming text messages and voicemails.

I pulled my sweater over my head and pulled off the blue jeans, leaving me covered in my camisole and soft pants as I picked up my phone, sat upon the edge of the bed, and sighed. Lying back, I hit the first voicemail message from my mother. The time stamp was yesterday afternoon.

"Julia, not returning our messages is childish. How can we be comfortable with your decisions when you're not replying?"

Listening to her dismissive and demeaning tone had the opposite effect of what her words intended. Closing my eyes, I let her message settle over me. As it did, I saw the errors of my ways, not recently, but in the past.

For the entirety of my life, I'd simply accepted my position in the family as the child. Despite my age signifying adulthood, I'd never exerted my independence. I'd never been encouraged to do so. My place was to accept my role as the Wade heir, as Mrs. Skylar Butler, and with taking over ownership of my stock of Wade—in name only.

It was never planned for me to be involved in the future of Wade Pharmaceutical. My father's recent confession confirmed as much.

Skipping three voicemails from my mother, I hit the screen to listen to the most recent, last night at near midnight.

"We're here, Julia. Come out of the house."

I exhaled as my stomach dropped.

My parents had been here at Van's home.

Are they still here in northern Wisconsin or have they gone home?

The text messages from both of my parents chronicled their flight to Ashland and their research that allowed them to find Van's address. There wasn't anything dubious about what they'd done. Donovan Sherman's address was public record.

Standing, I laid the phone on the bed, deciding to go downstairs and fill Van in on the identity of our visitors before my shower.

As I reached the door to the hallway, I heard the ring of my phone.

Begrudgingly, I turned around. "Fine, Mom. I'll talk to you," I spoke to no one, thinking how I hadn't ignored their messages or calls. I'd been outside of cell coverage. Approaching the bed, I decided not to tell her that. If she thought I was being childish, there wasn't anything I could say to change her mind.

The name upon the screen wasn't who I expected and immediately improved my disposition. The last time we'd spoken was when I told her the wedding was off.

Will I tell my friend that I have a new wedding on the horizon?

I answered, "Vicki."

"I'm worried about you. How are you doing?"

My cheeks rose higher. "I'm sure it sounds odd, but I'm good. I really am."

"There's so much I want to talk to you about," she said. "First, it's Christmas. I hate that you're alone."

"I'm not alone."

Her volume lowered. "I feel like this is the *Twilight Zone.* I saw a news bulletin about you and Skylar working out your differences."

"I promise that's not true."

She sighed. "I didn't think it was. Come back to Chicago. You can stay with me. We both know that your mom can be overbearing. You can hide out in my apartment and not even let your parents know you're in town. I just want you safe."

I sat back on the edge of the bed. Vicki knew my family, and she was right; Mom could be over-bearing. One of the things I loved about Victoria was that we'd been friends long enough that we knew most things about one another and our fami-lies. If life hadn't taken its most recent crazy turn with Van, I'd welcome her invitation. "I miss you, Vick."

"I miss you too. I feel like I've lost two of my best friends."

My curiosity got the better of me. "Have you spoken to Beth?"

"I have. I'm sorry."

"Don't be sorry. You and Beth are friends."

"So are you and Beth. She said she's tried to talk to you, leaving messages and texts. She saw the article about you and Skylar working it out."

"She should know that's not true."

"She doesn't; she says she's in limbo. She even called your mom."

I lay back on the bed. "I heard. Mom thinks I should call her."

"I don't," Vicki said. "She's my friend, but damn, it's not like she didn't tell you she was involved with just someone. She didn't tell you that she was involved with *Skylar*."

Tears I didn't expect burnt the back of my eyes. "In the long run, she saved me. I keep telling myself that. If Skylar would sleep around on me during our engagement, he would have done it after we married."

"He's scum," Vicki said definitively.

"I'm not sticking up for him, but I think that neither of us was in love with one another. We were just going forward on the road that was laid out for us when we were too young to question."

"The reason Beth doesn't know if the news is true or not is because Beth hasn't spoken to him since you left."

I sat up. "What?"

"He left town around the same time. He hasn't returned her calls. Mrs. Butler has been calling everyone to find him."

Where did he go after he left Ashland?

"Does Skylar's mom know that Beth is pregnant?" I asked.

Vicki's volume rose. "Oh, girl, I don't know, and if I were Beth, it sure as hell wouldn't be a discussion I'd want to have with the Butlers without Skylar's support."

Poor Beth.

Had I really just had that thought?

"When are you coming home?" Vicki asked.

"I got the job that I told you about. I'm going to stay here for a while."

She laughed. "That's another weird *Twilight Zone*-y thing. I knew you applied for a job, but yesterday, the crazy-ass newspeople have you engaged to someone else. It's wild. They twist everything." Before I could reply, she went on. "I looked the man up. He's uber rich and some good-looking recluse. I told my mom about it and said you'd gone for a job, not a new proposal."

"The job opportunity is why I came up here. The whole thing hasn't exactly worked out as I planned."

"Tell me about the job," Vicki said.

"The job is to write Donovan Sherman's memoir."

"That's the guy," she said, her voice rising. "I swear those reporters are crazy."

I sat taller. "They aren't. He did propose. I said yes."

"What the hell?"

I nodded. "I did. I know it's fast—"

"Lightning fast. I mean, he was good-looking, but isn't he too old for you?"

"Not as old as I expected when I went to the interview. His age doesn't bother me."

"Julia, you're really going to marry him? I don't approve."

"You don't?" I asked, surprised.

"I think he needs to meet your only best friend. Then we can discuss this."

My smile returned. "I'd love that. After the holidays when I go back to Chicago to gather my things."

Will Van go with me to Chicago?

I'd made the comment without thinking. After all, he was a successful man. He more than likely didn't have time to help me pack. Maybe I'd said he'd be there because I wanted him to be.

Vicki was talking. "You're moving up to northern Wisconsin? Really, Chicago doesn't get cold enough for you?"

"You wouldn't believe how cold it is here." Especially in a one-room cabin without electricity. I didn't say that last part because if I did, I'd admit other details about the last week to Vicki. That's what friends did.

It wasn't what Beth did.

By the time Vicki and I hung up, I changed my mind about going downstairs. My news regarding my parents could wait. Soon, I was under the warm spray of the shower, washing away the remains of Van's and my night and morning of passion.

Chapter 28

Julia

*S*till under the spray, I stilled as the bathroom door opened wide and Van appeared through the steam-covered glass stall. My hands crisscrossed my nakedness. "Van."

A smile filled his expression as he slid the glass door open. Reaching through the steam, he seized each of my hands. "What do you think you're hiding?"

The tenor of his voice rumbled through me as I relaxed my arms. "It's a reflex."

His green orbs simmered as he scanned from the top of my head to my toes. Even under the warm spray, my flesh peppered with goose bumps. His large finger came to the hickey upon my left breast, gently running over the bruise in small circles.

"I should leave more," he said, his eyes focused on the mark.

I reached for his hand. "Why are you here?"

"To see you, confirm you're real, and to remind

me how fucking fortunate I was to find you." Taking a breath, he pulled his attention away from my breast to my eyes. "What did you learn when you turned on your phone?"

I looked up at the shower spray and back. "Can this wait?"

"I wish. If it could, I'd step inside this stall right now."

"What's happening?"

"Your parents are on their way. They stayed in Ashland last night."

The joy I'd gotten from his decorated cabin for the holiday abandoned me, disappearing into the steam like a balloon losing air. "Did you invite them here?"

He nodded.

"Why?"

"Rinse." He reached for one of the plush towels. "And get out." His grin returned. "I'm pretty sure that meeting my future in-laws with their daughter naked and wearing my mark on her left breast and another on her right ass cheek won't be the best first impression."

My ass cheek?

What?

I twisted one way and the other, trying to see what was hidden.

Then his other words came through.

His future in-laws.

The thought of this impending meeting sent a feeling of dread through my circulation. I reached for the tile wall as Van took a step back and closed the glass door.

I waited for him to leave the bathroom but he didn't, leaning against the long vanity and crossing his arms over his wide chest.

"Are you going to give me a minute?" I asked.

"No. I'm going to enjoy the show."

Strip for me, beautiful.

The memory of that command twisted my core as I stepped back under the central spray, rinsing the conditioner from my hair. Of course, I was already bare, so stripping wasn't an issue. Instead, I rinsed, knowing his eyes were on me, watching, as I ran my own palms over my skin. It was his touch I felt on my breasts and his touch as my hands lowered.

Once the water was off, Van returned, towel in hand.

"How far away are they?" I asked as I took the towel.

"You have time to dry and dress."

I shook my head. "I don't want to see them."

His large hands framed my face. "Julia, it may not seem like it... There's a lot I don't know about you and your parents, but I'm willing to learn. What I do know is that you are in control."

"It's never felt that way."

"I can't answer why you have felt the way you have."

He turned us until we were standing before the large mirror. Despite my wet hair, I leaned back against his solid chest. The droplets from my hair dripped down my shoulders onto his thermal shirt, his boots, and the floor. The plush towel was wrapped around my breasts and hung to my thighs. Taller and wider, Van could be seen behind me, still dressed as he'd been in the cabin. The scent of the burning fire lingered in the fibers of his clothes. His jaw was covered with a day of beard growth, and his dark hair was wavy and unkempt from his sleep and his orange hat.

"Do you know what I see?" Van asked.

"A drowned rat."

His deep laugh filled the bathroom. "No. I see a strong woman."

"That's not what my parents see. They see their child. That's what they'll always see."

He lifted my wet hair and brought his lips to my neck. Such as lightning striking the surface of the earth, the energy of his kiss penetrated my skin, infiltrating my circulation, and racing through my nervous system. Closing my eyes, I tilted my head, giving Van more access.

"The only person who can change your parents' perception of you is you."

I spun and wrapped my arms around his torso. "I'm afraid they'll break our snow globe."

Van shook his head. "Our globe is unbreakable."

The definitiveness of his statement gave me strength. "I'm an adult."

"You definitely are."

I nodded. "Let me get dressed. I'll come down as fast as I can."

"Julia, I'm here for you. I could easily have handled this on the phone and forbade their coming to the house. I thought about it." He leaned down until his forehead met mine. "I have no problem being assertive. Truth be told, I have more trouble not being." Our eyes met. "My assertiveness won't facilitate what you want."

"What do I want?"

"To be seen as a capable adult in your parents' eyes."

I inhaled, knowing he was right.

"To achieve that outcome, you need to assert yourself. Show them that you can make your own decisions and let them know that you're aware of the consequences of those choices."

"I told them that you found me, that you saved me in the snowstorm. They said you're a rebound. You aren't."

Van nodded. "I know what I am. If I were your father instead of your fiancé, I wouldn't trust me. Don't get upset that they're leery. It only means that they care." He kissed the top of my head. "I'm not sure I trust them."

"What do you mean?"

"Wade was going down. How could your parents not know?"

I'd never thought of that.

As Van turned to leave, I called out his name.

He turned back.

"If you were my father," I asked, "and I came downstairs wearing a man's shirt, only his shirt, from a man I'd recently met and announced as my fiancé, what would you do?"

His grin returned, bringing gold shimmers to his green orbs. "I'd kill him."

"I'm serious."

"So am I. I don't mean mortally wound; I mean that I'd ruin him."

"I won't do it. I won't wear your shirt."

"Your dad can't ruin me. That's the difference. I could ruin him."

"But you won't," I said, wanting the reassurance.

"I'll do whatever you want, Julia. As I've said, my only connection or care for Wade Pharmaceutical is you."

"They're my parents."

He nodded. "Hurry, beautiful, they're on their way."

Standing in the large closet, I debated my few pieces of clothing. With my hair mostly dried and hanging over my shoulders and a minimal amount of makeup, I ran my fingers over the few pieces of clothes I had at my disposal. I could wear the outfit I'd worn to the interview or dress less formally and more laid-back. As I took in the soft sweaters, I decided for casual. After all, this was Christmas day and I was home.

Isn't that what Van wants me to think?

He'd said that he'd like me to refer to his home as mine. He'd said as his fiancée, nothing was off-limits.

Slipping on my heeled black boots, I took one more look in the mirror before leaving my suite. My soft black slacks and black tank top were covered with a long pink sweater. My hair was again piled on my head. Standing at the top of the staircase, I peered through the large window over the front door, wondering if my parents had arrived.

From the limited view of trees and sky it was impossible to know for sure. There were no voices below. A final destination called to me, a new curious thought. I peeked down the hallway toward Van's suite. The double doors were closed.

As my heart rate picked up its pace, I walked up the steps to the third floor.

My heartbeat thumped against my chest as I twisted the doorknob to the one door at the top of the stairs. To my surprise, the door opened inward. With only the waning light from the windows, I saw what Van had described—nothing. The large third-floor room was empty with two closed doors. I went to one, and opened it. The door led to a small bathroom. That too was empty. The fixtures were present, but there were no towels or paper products. Back out into the large open space, I opened the second door and stepped into what was a small room, a closet without clothes racks or shelves.

Flipping the switch within, I stared. Against the wall was a leaning stack of framed artwork. Apprehensively, I went closer, taking in the piece facing the door. I didn't recognize the artist's name, but the picture seemed familiar. One by one, I moved the frames, taking in each piece. The artists' names were different and some I'd heard before. All of the artwork was striking.

Why is it hidden away in an empty space?

Suddenly, my thoughts went back to my parents' impending visit. Stepping back into the empty room, I turned off the light and closed the door to the artwork, deciding that while I could eliminate one unknown about Van from my list—the emptiness of the third-floor room—I'd also added more questions.

As I came to the top of the staircase going down

to the main level, my pulse drummed in my ears as the reverberating sound of the piano floated to the level above.

I held my breath as the rich notes resonated through the entry.

Quietly, I made my way down the stairs, stopping on the bottom step and holding tightly to the banister. Closing my eyes, I listened to the melancholy melody as each note struck a string within my heart. If this were a movie, the chosen soundtrack would give me an ominous feel leading into our planned meeting.

Walking softly, I entered the living room.

The sun beyond the windows had begun to sink below the horizon. Despite the relatively early hour, darkness was about to fall. A fire roared within the large hearth and the aroma of Mrs. Mayhand's holiday meal could be smelled from the kitchen.

Van's eyes were closed as his fingers ran over the keys. It was as if he had a sixth sense, feeling the piano instead of seeing it. His hands worked independently from one another as his toes pressed the appropriate pedals and his wide shoulders and torso swayed with the beat.

The mountain-man clothes from before were replaced by casual wear, faded blue jeans, canvas loafers, and a long-sleeved button-up with his sleeves rolled to his elbows. His damp dark hair and clean-shaven jaw told me that he'd showered after coming into my bathroom.

The melody slowed as his eyes opened.

His expression that only seconds before seemed sad morphed before my eyes as his green stare met mine.

"That was beautiful," I said, walking up to the large piano. "Please don't stop."

"I like when you say that—not to stop." He tilted his head to the side, indicating the bench beside him.

Standing at his side, I ran my palm over his smooth cheek. "You know, if you were going to shower, you could have joined me."

"We'd still be up there."

"There's always later tonight."

Sitting where he'd indicated, I peered up at his protruding brow. "Are you worried about this meeting?"

"Why do you ask?"

"You said you haven't played the piano in a while and that song was ominous."

"I haven't played." He spun, pulling one leg over the bench and tugging me between his legs. "I seem to mostly remember morose melodies. I should brush up on some happier songs."

"When did you say you stopped playing?"

He shrugged. "I don't think I said." When I didn't

speak, he answered. "It was before Brooklyn was born."

"Have you tried to speak to your brother?"

He shook his head. "Let's concentrate on one family at a time. I'll get a notification when your parents pass the gate."

"Did you close it?"

"No, it's electronically monitored. I didn't have my phone turned on at the cabin and there's no Wi-Fi or cell service out there. That's why last night I didn't realize the barrier had been breached."

My chest pushed against my sweater as I inhaled. "I want them to come and go so we can be just us."

Van's large hands roamed up and down my arms, finding my skin beneath the large openings of the sweater cuffs. "I would tell your parents to leave and keep you hidden if I could."

My forehead fell to his wide chest. "I would like that."

His chest inflated as his expression became unreadable. "Hidden away for only me" —his grasp of my waist tightened— "my private obsession." He shook his head. "That wouldn't be right. You'd retaliate..."

"Van?" I looked up as his stare reached deep inside me.

"I've done some bad things," Van said. "I want everything to be different with you, Julia. I won't hide you from your family, but if you ever want me to intervene, I will. You say the word." He left a kiss on my hair. "You think I'm old."

"I didn't say—"

His finger came to my lips. "I'm not, but I've screwed up enough to know what's right and what isn't. For this to work, for us to work," he clarified, "you have to be an active partner."

A smile curled my lips. "I tried at the cabin."

"You did great. I don't mean just with sex. I mean, for your parents to believe this—what's happening between you and me—is real, they need to hear it from you. They have no reason to trust me and probably many reasons not to trust me. They trust you."

I inhaled and straightened my neck, feeling the weight of the responsibility I'd failed to accept, that I'd avoided taking, and that Van was presenting to me.

He was right.

For too long I'd been willing to let others speak for me. Whether it was my mother, father, or Skylar, I allowed it. Van wasn't saying he'd abandon me. He was saying that I needed to use my voice. It was the encouragement I'd never before had.

"You're right," I admitted.

"If you want me to step in, let me know."

"They need to hear it from me."

His warm touch skirted my arms. "What are you going to say?"

"I'll tell them the truth. You and I are engaged. I'm going to marry you. The date isn't set, but I've said yes. And as for Wade, you will help."

"I'll do what you want." He looked down at his watch. "Someone has crossed the gate line."

Chapter 29

Julia

 $\mathcal{V}$ an opened the door to the entry and we stepped beyond the glass French doors. Through the sidelights we could gaze out onto the driveway. The SUV was parked facing the south wing, as the doors began to open—three of them. My stomach sank and I reached for Van's hand. His body stiffened beside mine.

"Fuck," Van muttered under his breath.

I could barely articulate what was happening. "They brought Skylar."

My father had said he'd tell him off and now Skylar was with them.

The threesome stood still for a moment on the driveway, doing as I'd done upon my first arrival, taking in the sheer size of Van's home. As if on cue, the floodlights illuminated the area. I turned to Van in question.

"Light sensor."

Dad, Mom, and Skylar turned in all directions,

squinting as they took in the sudden influx of light.

"I can tell them the invitation is revoked," Van offered. He squeezed my hand. "If you're going to marry me, you'll learn fast; I have no issues with being the asshole."

My neck straightened. "No. You were right before. I need to face them. I've already faced Skylar, but screw him. If two rejections weren't enough for him" —I was thinking of when I left the ring with the note and then also our conversation at the hotel bar in Ashland— "I'll be happy to give him a repeat performance."

As the three of them began to walk toward the solid large door, Van reached for my chin and brought his lips to mine. The kiss was chaste and quick, leaving a smile on my face.

"I have your back, but you don't need me."

I blinked away the prickle of tears. "I think I do, Van. I think you're exactly what I've needed. I just didn't know it."

He took a deep breath as the chime of the ringing doorbell echoed through the entry and beyond. Taking a step forward, he opened the door. From my perspective, I saw the surprise in the three sets of eyes; undoubtedly, they'd expected someone else, perhaps a housekeeper or maid. That was who would have answered the door at either my parents' home or Skylar's parents'.

"Mr. Sherman," my father said, being the first to speak.

Van took a step back, "Mr. McGrath, Mrs. McGrath..." He paused long enough to punctuate his greeting with an added bit of unease. "...and Mr. Butler." He nodded toward Skylar. "An unexpected surprise."

From my vantage, I found it odd the way the three of them were looking at Van, odd and also interesting, as if they were all intimidated by his mere presence. Maybe they were.

Would I feel differently about Van if I'd meet him under different circumstances?

"Mr. Sherman," they all acknowledged as they came through the door.

My mother was the first to address me, coming closer and wrapping me in an embrace. "I needed to see you."

"Here I am."

For the first time I could recall, I found myself skeptical of her glassy eyes and the sincerity in her voice. I couldn't explain how they felt orchestrated when they never had before, but nevertheless, that's the way they felt.

She gripped my shoulders, staring directly into my eyes. "We have so many things to discuss." She peered over her shoulder at Van and back. "Come with us. These are family matters."

My gaze met Van's. It wasn't a lingering stare or even long enough to enjoy the depth of his emerald orbs with their flickering gold flecks. It was enough to bolster my strength.

I opened the French doors to the house. "You're here. Come inside, we can talk here—and once we're married, Van will be family. Skylar on the other hand..." I let the rest go unsaid.

Mom went inside.

Standing my ground as sentry, I waited as Mom's blue eyes darted from here to there as she took in the surroundings. Van's home wasn't as opulently decorated as our home. The limestone structure in Lincoln Park was maintained as if it were a stop on the historical-house tour. It wasn't. My mother would loathe having strangers enter her home and trample her expensive rugs. Yet the contrast was as obvious as cold versus warm.

Where my childhood home appeared cold and staged to an outsider, it was impossible not to feel the metaphoric warmth of Van's home, the woodwork, furnishings, and literal warmth of the huge fireplace.

Dad stopped before passing me, reaching for my hand and giving it a squeeze. "I've missed you, little girl."

His familiar address wasn't upsetting.

Some things went without saying. One day when I was a grandmother, I'd still be my father's little girl.

I held my breath as the last of the trio passed me. Skylar's lips appeared glued together in a straight line as he walked past Van and then me, his blue eyes fixed on the room ahead.

Van's hand came to the small of my back, finding its way between the sweater and tank top beneath. "You've got this," he whispered.

Soon the five of us were in the living room.

"Please, have a seat," I said, "and I suppose if you plan to stay, you can take off your coats."

"I'll take them," Van offered, gathering the coats and laying them upon a chair closer to the entry.

His choice of location was all the better for them to grab on their way out. The thought made me smile.

Them leaving.

Van and I alone.

"Surely, you have help," Mom said as she handed Van her coat. "This is too much house for one man."

Van grinned as he replied. "Thankfully, my lonely days *and nights* are over."

Mom's neck straightened.

I'd been too busy watching her to see Dad's or Skylar's response.

"Mr. Sherman," Dad began.

Van again gestured toward the sofas before the fireplace. "Please, as Julia said, sit. It's Christmas, and I'm sure you have places to be. As you can tell by the delicious aroma in the air, Julia and I have dinner waiting." He shrugged. "Had we had advance notice, we would have had more food for us all to enjoy."

So that's why Van started the meal.

I could live with that.

Mom, Dad, Van, and I sat as Skylar, still wearing his overcoat, walked to the tall windows. The bay beyond was veiled in darkness, yet the scene seemed to hold his attention. I had a sudden memory of the smudge that Margaret had found so unusual, and in a childish way, I wished for its reappearance, right where Skylar was standing.

"This recent change in plans came suddenly," Mom said.

I sat taller. "Skylar's impending parenthood—is that what you're talking about?"

From the corner of my eye, I saw Skylar turn. His voice boomed throughout the open space. "She lied, Julia. Beth isn't pregnant."

I knew that wasn't true from my conversation with Vicki. Or at least I knew Beth had been pregnant. Her current status wasn't my concern.

"The cancellation of the wedding wasn't sudden," I said, speaking to both of them. "It was overdue."

"Your mother means," Dad offered, "what is happening here."

Turning to Van, I took in his confident grin. In that second, I saw the man he told me he could be. I saw the qualities in his eyes. Van would let me handle this, he'd encouraged me to handle this, yet at no time was he unprepared. There was a calm calculation in his expression. He may have been surprised by Skylar's presence, but he was nonetheless equipped to handle wherever this discussion went.

If I were to guess, I'd say that Van was prepared before he offered the invitation for their arrival.

Who I currently saw was the man whose memoir I had been hired to write. He was the wolf on Wall Street, the predator who seeks out wounded companies and businesses, and the man at the top who alone determines the fate of those within his sights.

"What is happening here," I offered, sitting near the edge of the leather chair, "is cosmic irony. I came to Ashland without knowing the identity of the man advertising for someone to pen his memoir. I didn't expect to end up in a blizzard or a snowbank. I certainly didn't know who rescued me."

"Or where the white ribbon would lead," Van added.

Seemingly ignoring Van's comment, my mother pleaded, "Julia, Skylar asked to come with us to apologize to you in person and explain that Beth isn't carrying his child."

I shook my head. "Thank you, Mom."

"For?"

"For speaking for Skylar. I've noticed his inability

to say more than a few words since his arrival. He's fortunate to have you here to articulate his feelings."

"I-I'm not—"

"Oh, but you are." I stood. "It's what you do. You probably have already conveyed my feelings in return. However, you forgot to ask me what they are. Tell me, am I willing to listen to his apology for sleeping with my best friend?" Before she could respond, I went on, "My thoughts regarding Beth's pregnancy state is that regardless of her current status or" —I turned toward Skylar— "the accuracy of the text message I read, it doesn't matter."

"Right," Mom said. "It doesn't. You have a life in Chicago, not here in this godforsaken wilderness."

I suppressed a smile, thinking of the cabin. Van's home wasn't a godforsaken wilderness. If only my mother could see the cabin. My attention stayed on my mother. "No," I said matter-of-factly. "What doesn't matter is Beth's pregnancy status or what it was. It matters that she claimed Skylar was the father and he didn't deny the possibility." I turned to my ex-fiancé. "If returning the engagement ring and our subsequent conversation at the hotel didn't make it clear enough for you, I don't accept your apology. We can't work this out."

"You don't know the truth about him," Skylar said, his chin pointing toward Van.

Shaking my head at his pathetic attempt to

attribute blame, I looked at Mom. "You said there's more to marriage than love. You're right. There's trust and fidelity. I won't walk into a marriage without those fundamental elements."

"And yet," Mother replied, "you agreed to marry Mr. Sherman."

Van was sitting back, with his ankle resting on one knee. His eyes moved from Mother to me and back as if he were watching a tennis match, waiting for the game-winning point to be scored.

"Yes, I did."

"When?" Dad asked.

"We haven't set a date."

"So you plan to live here in sin?" Mother asked.

Red sin.

I didn't try to hide my smile. "I have my own suite."

"If you expect us to believe..." Skylar spoke from near the windows.

"I don't give a shit what you believe," I said, my volume rising. "It's none of your business. You lost all rights as far as I am concerned when you screwed my friend." I took a breath. "But I won't lie to any of you."

Van lowered his leg, sitting forward.

"I'm more content with Van than I ever imagined I could be, ever. In the short time we've been together, he's shown me that I have a voice." I turned to Mom. "One you've successfully stifled over the years."

"You're only twenty-four years old," she said.

"I'm legally an adult. I can make my own decisions and I have."

Dad motioned for me to sit. "You're right."

"I am?" I didn't mean for it to come out as a question.

"You can make decisions. Just because you can make these decisions," Dad said with an element of calm my mother lacked, "doesn't mean that they're the right ones. That isn't your fault. You don't have all the information on Mr. Sherman. He has a reputation he may not have shared with you."

"I'm sure there are many things about Van that I don't know." I turned toward him, seeing his gaze that I'd felt from my first word. "And I'm willing to take a lifetime to learn them."

"Did he tell you that he's now secured another five of the remaining fifteen percent of Wade shares?" Dad asked.

I turned to Van.

Without a word and from the expression on Van's face, I knew what my father said was true. I wanted to question Van and learn the details, but I also refused to expose a possible kink in the security of our snow globe to my parents.

"You didn't know, did you?" Dad asked.

"I didn't," I replied honestly. "However, I have Van's word that my wishes will be upheld regarding Wade. I trust him and his word."

"My father doesn't," Skylar said. "He sent me an interesting file on Mr. Thomas."

The use of Van's original last name had little effect on Van, and more on me. "I don't care what your father said. He wanted to sell Wade. He was going to take control while we were on our honeymoon. By the time we returned, he could have the entire company liquidated."

"That's not what Dad was going to do," Skylar said, coming closer. "The shares he had lined up were our wedding present. I knew about them, Jules. It was only a secret from you. Your parents knew. Mom and Dad wanted to give us overarching control. Our future would have been secure. Now, Sherman owns twenty-six percent—one more percent than the Butlers. Why would he do that?"

A wedding present?

Before I could reply, Van spoke to my father. "What is your concern, Mr. McGrath?"

"My concern is for my daughter."

"Your daughter is in good hands, I assure you. What is your concern regarding Wade Pharmaceutical?"

Chapter 30

Van

"We want it to survive. My grandfather created—"

Mr. McGrath's hand came up, silencing his wife. It was a welcome gesture, but one I was surprised she heeded. "For the record," Julia's father said, "I'm still concerned about Julia. She's young and you're..."

"I'm older," I admitted. "I'm not concerned about Julia's youth. She's an amazingly quick study."

Over the crackling of the fire, there was a collective inhale. Yes, I'd hit a chord and I would be happy to hit more. "What is your concern regarding Wade?" I asked again.

"The unknown is rattling the shareholders."

I nodded. "We're down to fewer and fewer when it comes to shareholders. Currently, there is you" —I nodded toward Mr. McGrath— "maintaining Julia's shares, the Butlers, roughly four or five other entities holding ten percent, and myself." I sat back against the chair. "Tell me who is rattled, and I'll be happy to take their shares off their hands."

"Why would you do that?" Mrs. McGrath asked. "Wade Pharmaceutical is nothing with a portfolio like yours. You could easily ruin us and leave the company for dust, a write-off."

"He won't," Julia said.

"Mr. Sherman?" Mr. McGrath asked. "Why should we trust you?"

"You don't have to. Don't trust me. Your shares will be mine once Julia and I are married." Before he could protest, I waved him off. "Yes, of course there will be a prenuptial agreement. However, theoretically, they'll be at my disposal. I'm working on the other ten percent. That will give Julia and me sixty-five to seventy-five percent." I turned to the dickass by the window. "Sell me your shares, Mr. Butler. I'll pay double what they're currently worth."

Skylar Butler turned my way.

I could read him like an old newspaper. He was seeing money signs and opportunity. Wade didn't mean anything to him. He wasn't attached, yet he couldn't show that tonight, not here in front of Julia and her parents.

"No," he finally said. "Wade has a sentimental value. I work there as does my father."

"Sell to me and you can quit."

It was Julia's turn to stare in silence, her gaze

going between me, her fiancé, and dickass, her ex-fiancé.

"The Butlers aren't selling," Mrs. McGrath said.

Her answer made me scoff. It was exactly as Julia had said; Mrs. McGrath spoke for whomever she wanted. Ignoring her interruption, I spoke to Butler. "Think about it, and if you decide to have an opinion of your own, call me. My people will draw up the paperwork."

"I have an opinion," he said meekly.

I could cut him up and have him for lunch. If he'd learned his skills from his father, either Marlin had been a horrible teacher or he wasn't interested in teaching his son the finer art of business negotiation. There was also no way on earth I would pay double the value to the Butlers. This performance was simply for the enjoyment of watching Butler squirm and providing entertainment to the McGraths.

I turned back to Julia's father. "Sir, as long as Julia wants Wade to succeed, it will. By buying up the available shares, my hope is to return Wade to the status it enjoyed prior to Herman Wade's decision to sell shares. Wade would be more of a reckoning force if it were back to a privately held company without outside influence."

The answer was in Mr. McGrath's eyes. I'd just offered him a deal he could live with, what he'd strived for since taking the co-CEO position.

"We have debt," he said. "We still have a January 3rd date to either produce a balloon payment that we can't afford or to accept a crippling increased interest rate."

"Gregg," Mrs. McGrath scolded.

"What, Ana? If you don't think a man like Mr. Sherman knows everything there is to know about Wade, then you're the one who's delusional."

I spoke, "I was aware of the January 3rd deadline even before you told Julia and she told me. I do my homework."

"We can't make it—the balloon payment," Mr. McGrath said, his head shaking. "We'll have to accept the increase in interest." He exhaled and leaned forward. "That too is too much for us to pay. We won't make it."

"What are you saying, Dad?" Julia asked. "Is it too late?"

"No, it's not," Mrs. McGrath said. "The combination of McGrath and Butler has been planned forever. This was going to restore Wade's standing. Once our rating was higher, the interest rates would lower."

"That scenario isn't happening. Do you have a backup plan for raising your standing?" I asked.

The McGraths looked at one another. Finally, it was Julia's father who spoke. "We have researchers working on an Alzheimer's medication that, if the clinical trials go well, will be able to be produced for much less than the one currently applying for approval."

"I hadn't heard about that," I admitted, intrigued.

"Because we haven't announced it," Julia's mother said. "There are advantages to being small. We stay under the radar until we want to be seen."

"Will you send me your research?"

She sat straighter. "Are you also a biophysicist, Mr. Sherman?"

"No, Mrs. McGrath, I'm a businessman. The shares I just purchased...had those stockholders been made aware of this new medication on the horizon?"

"No," Butler said, joining the conversation. "It was my father's belief that if we announced too soon and the wider studies didn't come out as the earlier and smaller controlled studies had, it would hurt us."

Marlin Butler knew about the possible future profitability of Wade and chose not to disclose it to the people whose stock he'd arranged to purchase. I wondered if he'd sold the new medication idea to the bigger companies he was courting. That could definitely increase the value of his shares.

"How long until the wider studies will have data to share with the CDC and FDA?" Julia asked.

A smile curled my lips as I watched her take part in this conversation.

Her father answered. "Unfortunately, we can't

know that for sure." He turned to me. "We just need to hang on."

My entrepreneurial interest in controlling shares of Wade Pharmaceutical was increasing by the minute. I turned to Julia. "What do you think?"

"She doesn't have the information," her mother interjected.

"I can speak for myself," Julia said. "I don't have the information. I want it. Send me everything and to Van too. The recent upheaval has made me realize that I do care about Wade. This new information makes me hopeful that I'm not simply asking Van to save a failing company, but that by saving it, we could see the fortunes turn."

"My father won't agree to sending the data," Butler said. "It's all in-house. We can't risk a leak."

It was on the tip of my tongue to tell this runt what I thought of him and his father. Before I could, Julia stepped in.

"Marlin has a say as long as he maintains his twenty-five percent. That's all he has, Skylar—a twenty-five-percent say. As I said at the hotel, don't push me. If you do, I'll make sure you, your father, and your uncle are permanently removed from the day-to-day running of Wade."

Logan is involved?

In what capacity?

He wasn't listed as a stockholder, board member,

or anywhere among the employee information.

"You can't do that," Butler said.

"Julia has a say, too," Mr. McGrath said. "The McGrath shares will be under her jurisdiction upon her marriage."

I was awed by Julia's expression, seeing the way she internalized her father's acknowledgment of her position.

"Not to him," Butler said, his chin coming my way. "Julia is kidding herself if she thinks she'll have a say with him. He won't listen. She's handing Wade to the enemy."

"How is Van the enemy?" Julia asked.

Her father spoke, "I think it's best to keep tempers out of this. Right now, it's business."

"Your father wants to sell," Julia said.

"No," Butler rebutted. "I told you that his plan was to give the shares to us."

Standing, I reached for Julia's hand and spoke to her parents. "It was nice to meet you."

The McGraths both stood, recognizing the cue I'd given for them to leave.

"Hopefully, by this time next year, we can celebrate together as a family. If you'll excuse us, I don't want our dinner to be overdone."

"Please come home," Mrs. McGrath said to Julia. "There is no rush for this...wedding."

"Not for the wedding, but there is a rush," Julia

said. "The bank wants the balloon payment by the third." Her blue eyes came to me. "Van is our only hope in making that payment. I can't and won't ask him to do that without him knowing I'm steadfast in my decision to marry him. He deserves that."

"You can reassure him from Chicago," her mother said.

"No, Mom, I'm staying. I'm marrying Van, writing his story, and taking a more active role at Wade." Before anyone could comment, she looked at me and grinned. "Sixty-five to seventy-five percent."

I nodded.

"Julia…" Her mother's plea faded away.

Julia turned to her mother. "Merry Christmas, Mom and Dad. I love you. That hasn't changed, but I have." She looked down to where our hands were connected. "Whether Van entering my life was fate or red sin, he's shown me in this short time that I have a voice and I can use it."

"You've always had a voice."

"No, Mom. I've always gone along with yours. Grandpa's will gives me power. Van's encouragement has given me the strength to assert it."

Mr. McGrath offered me his hand. "Mr. Sherman, my daughter is my single greatest joy. Keeping Wade afloat has been my greatest struggle. I don't know you, but if you're sincere, I hope you're right, and in a year, we can be one family."

Releasing Julia, I shook his hand.

Julia went to her mother and offered her a hug. "Bye, Mom. I'll be in touch after the first of the year."

Mrs. McGrath hesitated. "I don't want to leave you here all alone."

"I'm not alone."

"I do my homework too," Butler announced.

All eyes turned to him.

"If you have something to say," I said, "we're listening."

He spoke to Julia. "You want information, I'll send you information."

"If you have something to say," Julia repeated, "say it. I'm done with this fake reconciliation."

"Sherman is lying to you," Butler said. "Dad has known him since before his name was Sherman."

"I'm well aware of his name change," Julia said. "That isn't news."

Mr. McGrath motioned to Butler. "It's time that we leave."

After a few more tense goodbyes and Butler whispering something to Julia, she and I stood in the entry and watched as all three got back into the SUV. I wrapped my arm around her. "You did wonderfully."

Her smile beamed up at me. "Because I knew I wasn't alone. You were here with me. And my dad actually listened."

"You are a powerhouse, Julia. I believe in you."

Chapter 31

Julia

Back in the kitchen, I reached for the oven mitts and opened the top wall oven, removing the turkey breast. The second oven contained the casseroles to complete our holiday meal.

"What did Butler whisper before he left?" Van asked.

I shook my head. "It doesn't matter. Let's celebrate. My parents are gone and this is our first Christmas."

Van's smile returned. "The first item on that list definitely deserves celebration."

As I arranged the dishes, Van pulled a bottle of wine from the rack and brought down two glasses. My mind was on what Skylar had said.

I knew I shouldn't give Skylar or his ideas the time of day, but what he'd mentioned wasn't new. It was something I'd already wondered about. It was also the subject that Mrs. Mayhand had commented about, saying that some questions were better not asked.

Van handed me a glass of wine and lifted his own. "To our guests leaving."

A smile curled my lips as I stared at him, deep into his emerald eyes, and brought my glass to his. "To us being alone."

Our glasses clinked before we both took a sip.

A few minutes later before we had the opportunity to sit, our food plated and wine glasses refilled and on the table, Van reached for my hand. "I want to tell you every day that you amaze me because you do."

"I didn't make this meal."

"No," he said, the gold flecks in his orbs shimmering under the kitchen lights. "You did so much more. You stood up for yourself, and I couldn't be prouder."

He wrapped his arms around me, pulling me against his solid strength and to the place I wanted to be. Van had become that to me. He'd become my place of restoration, whether here in this big house, in the cabin, or in the wilderness. Within his presence, I felt at peace.

And yet there was a lingering question.

I looked up. "Van, who is Madison?"

The muscles of his torso tightened as his head tilted to the side. "Why are you asking?"

"Skylar said something. I don't want to believe him." I shook my head, still keeping my arms wrapped around Van. "After all, I have all the reason in the world not to believe him. I believe you. Why is your company called Sherman and Madison?"

He inhaled. "Once you go through all the information, you'll learn that Madison was a friend and I chose to honor that friendship."

"Just a friend?"

Inhaling, he shook his head.

"I'm not asking as the writer," I said. "I'm asking as your fiancée. Who is Madison?" I said a silent prayer that Skylar had lied. After all, it couldn't be true. The pieces didn't fit.

Van's voice was deadpan as he answered, shattering our snow globe, "My wife."

* * *

Thank you for beginning the journey on the "White Ribbon" and plunging into RED SIN.
You won't want to miss a moment of Van and Julia's story as more twists and turns and sexy times come along with book two of the Sin Series, GREEN ENVY.

If you enjoyed *RED SIN*, you can also check out the recently completed DEVIL'S Series Duet, beginning with the free prequel "Fate's Demand" and book one *DEVIL'S DEAL*.

Do you enjoy dangerous, mafia romance? If you do, you don't want to miss KINGDOM COME, an all new stand-alone romance.

Turn back to *Books by Aleatha* for a complete and up-to-date listing of all the stories Aleatha has to offer.

WHAT TO DO NOW

LEND IT: Did you enjoy RED SIN? Do you have a friend who'd enjoy RED SIN? RED SIN may be lent one time. Sharing is caring!

RECOMMEND IT: Do you have multiple friends who'd enjoy my dark romance with twists and turns and an all new sexy and mysterious anti-hero? Tell them about the Sin Series! Call, text, post, tweet...your recommendation is the nicest gift you can give to an author!

REVIEW IT: Tell the world. Please go to the retailer where you purchased this book, as well as Goodreads, and write a review. Please share your thoughts about RED SIN on:

*Amazon, RED SIN Customer Reviews

*Barnes & Noble, RED SIN, Customer Reviews

*Apple Books, RED SIN Customer Reviews

* BookBub, RED SIN Customer Reviews

*Goodreads.com/Aleatha Romig

Books by ALEATHA

RIBBON SERIES:

WHITE RIBBON

August 2021

RED SIN

October 2021

GREEN ENVY

January 2022

UNDERWORLD KINGS:

KINGDOM COME

DEVIL'S SERIES (Duet):

Prequel: "FATES DEMAND"

March 18

DEVIL'S DEAL

May 2021

ANGEL'S PROMISE

June 2021

WEB OF SIN:

SECRETS

October 2018

LIES

December 2018

PROMISES

January 2019

TANGLED WEB:

TWISTED

May 2019

OBSESSED

July 2019

BOUND

August 2019

WEB OF DESIRE:

SPARK

Jan. 14, 2020

FLAME

February 25, 2020

ASHES

April 7, 2020

DANGEROUS WEB:

Prequel: "Danger's First Kiss"

DUSK

November 2020

DARK

January 2021

DAWN

February 2021

* * *

THE INFIDELITY SERIES:

BETRAYAL

Book #1

October 2015

CUNNING

Book #2

January 2016

DECEPTION

Book #3

May 2016

ENTRAPMENT

Book #4

September 2016

FIDELITY

Book #5

January 2017

* * *

THE CONSEQUENCES SERIES:

CONSEQUENCES

(Book #1)

August 2011

TRUTH

(Book #2)

October 2012

CONVICTED

(Book #3)

October 2013

REVEALED

(Book #4)

Previously titled: Behind His Eyes Convicted: The Missing Years

June 2014

BEYOND THE CONSEQUENCES

(Book #5)

January 2015

RIPPLES (Consequences stand-alone)

October 2017

CONSEQUENCES COMPANION READS:

BEHIND HIS EYES-CONSEQUENCES

January 2014

BEHIND HIS EYES-TRUTH

March 2014

* * *

STAND ALONE MAFIA THRILLER:

PRICE OF HONOR

Available Now

* * *

THE LIGHT DUET:

Published through Thomas and Mercer Amazon exclusive

INTO THE LIGHT

June 2016

AWAY FROM THE DARK

October 2016

* * *

TALES FROM THE DARK SIDE SERIES:

INSIDIOUS

(All books in this series are stand-alone erotic thrillers)

Released October 2014

* * *

ALEATHA'S LIGHTER ONES:

PLUS ONE

Stand-alone fun, sexy romance

May 2017

ANOTHER ONE

Stand-alone fun, sexy romance

May 2018

ONE NIGHT

Stand-alone, sexy contemporary romance

September 2017

A SECRET ONE

April 2018

* * *

INDULGENCE SERIES:

UNEXPECTED

August 2018

UNCONVENTIONAL

January 2018

UNFORGETTABLE

October 2019

UNDENIABLE

August 2020

About the AUTHOR

Aleatha Romig is a New York Times, Wall Street Journal, and USA Today bestselling author who lives in Indiana, USA. She has raised three children with her high school sweetheart and husband of over thirty years. Before she became a full-time author, she worked days as a dental hygienist and spent her nights writing. Now, when she's not imagining mind-blowing twists and turns, she likes to spend her time with her family and friends. Her other pastimes include reading and creating heroes/anti-heroes who haunt your dreams!

Aleatha impresses with her versatility in writing. She released her first novel, CONSEQUENCES, in August of 2011. CONSEQUENCES, a dark romance, became a bestselling series with five novels and two companions released from 2011 through 2015. The compelling and epic story of Anthony and Claire Rawlings has graced more than half a million e-readers. Her first stand-alone smart, sexy thriller INSIDIOUS was next. Then Aleatha released the five-novel INFIDELITY series, a romantic suspense saga, that took the reading world by storm, the final book landing on three of the top bestseller lists. She ventured into traditional publishing with Thomas and Mercer. Her books INTO THE LIGHT and AWAY FROM THE DARK were published through this mystery/thriller publisher in 2016. In the spring of 2017, Aleatha again ventured into a different genre with her first fun and sexy stand-alone romantic comedy with the USA Today bestseller PLUS ONE. She continued with ONE NIGHT and ANOTHER ONE. If you like fun, sexy, novellas that make your heart pound, try her INDULGENCE SERIES. In 2018 Aleatha returned to her dark romance roots with SPARROW WEBS.

Aleatha is a "Published Author's Network" member of the Romance Writers of America, PEN America, and NINC. She is represented by Kevan Lyon of Marsal Lyon Literary Agency and Dani Sanchez with Wildfire Marketing.

facebook.com/aleatharomig

twitter.com/aleatharomig

instagram.com/aleatharomig